"Just who are these Christians anyway?"

By Gearoid Griffin.

A fanciful tale of the Irish man who prefigured St. Patrick.

© Gearoid Griffin 2024

All rights reserved. No part of this publication may be reproduced, stored in a retrieval system or transmitted in any form or by any means, electronic, mechanical, photocopying, recording or otherwise without the prior written permission of the publisher.

This book is sold subject to the condition that it shall not, by way of trade or otherwise, be lent, resold, hired out without the publisher's prior consent in any form of binding or cover other than that in which it is published and without a similar condition including this condition being imposed on the subsequent purchaser.

For my neighbours and friends,
and
all God's children
in Aughrim
and
in its beautiful rugged sylvan surrounds.

Also by Gearoid Griffin:
Why humankind? – "*this and that*".
After Noon on the Sixth Day.

"JUST WHO ARE THESE CHRISTIANS, ANYWAY?"

(A Roman newspaper series of articles)

Publisher's note:
In the first century C.E. Ireland, an island at the extreme west of the known world was known as "*Hibernia*". It was not part of the Roman Empire. Some three hundred years earlier it had been invaded and conquered by Celts from central Europe. They brought with them knowledge of iron working and created a Gaelic culture dominated by warlords with their fiefdoms (known as *Túathaí*) and by Druids. It was here in the year 26 C.E. that Dónal Questor was born in a ringfort called Bóthar na gCloch (road of the stones) which was bordered on three sides by steep cliffs and was the fort of Cú Roí Mac Daire, a great king and warrior. It was situated near the present-day town of Annascaul in Kerry. Dónal's father, Felix Questor had been a sailor on a Roman Trireme which had been surveying the west coast of Albion with a view to that country's annexation by Rome. The boat foundered and sank in a storm in the Irish sea and he had haphazardly made his way to Kerry. Felix somehow inveigled his way into the household of the local king. He hand-fasted (that is, married) a daughter of a leading Druid. They prospered and had seven children of whom Dónal was the youngest and his father's favourite. It was Felix who taught Latin and Greek to Dónal and cultivated in him a great curiosity about the empire and, particularly, *"Imperium sine fine,"* and Rome, thus kindling in Dónal a wanderlust to see its magnificence for himself.

In the year 45 C.E. word reached Dónal in Bóthar na gCloch that Albion had fallen under the sway of Rome. Surely the Romans would now try to conquer Hibernia, the last outpost of the world. While Dónal had a great desire to see the great city of Rome he was totally opposed to the notion of his kingdom being ruled by any other kingdom or nation, a sentiment shared vehemently by all of the many Túathí. The rite of passage for all young men in Hibernia entailed some years spent training to become one of the Fianna[1] and emulate the legendary Fionn mac Cumhaill.[2] Dónal, with his father's blessing, and along with thousands of other young warriors made his way to the east coast to repel any potential incursion by

---
[1] The *Fianna* way of life involved living in the wild, hunting, raiding, martial and athletic training, and even training in poetry. They also served as mercenaries.
[2] Fionn mac Cumhaill was the legendary Irish warrior/hunter who led the band of Irish warriors known as the Fianna and is said to have created the Giant's Causeway.

Roman armies. The ferocity of their resistance and their pursuit of the Romans even on to the coastal areas of Albion perplexed the Roman generals and soon dissuaded them of entertaining aspirations to occupy Hibernia.

Through a fantastic series of adventures and misadventures (which are recounted in his biography, *"A Hibernian, a Roman and an Inquirer."*) Dónal found himself in Rome and, at age 28, working as a reporter for Rome's paramount weekly chronicle.

Claudius was emperor when Dónal reached Rome. There were plenty of sensational stories to be reported. Claudius' wife, Messalina was promiscuous with a penchant for servants – but, could you put that in a newspaper? When she took up with Gaius Sillius the cruel Claudius had them killed without batting an eyelid – it is said that when news of their deaths reached him, he simply asked for more wine! Put that in the papers and you die. Claudius then married his own niece, Agrippina. From the frying pan of Messalina into the fire of Agrippina! She *"removed"* "all of her potential rivals, got Claudius to disinherit his own son so that her son, Nero became the only heir. The stage was set. She then fed Claudius poisoned mushrooms. But Claudius began to recover from the poison. The doctor was summoned to minister to the emperor. However, Agrippina induced the doctor to administer further poison to Claudius.

The year was 54 – Nero aged 17 was now emperor – matters would not improve.

Nero, a man with light blue eyes, thick neck, protruding stomach, and spindly legs, was a crazed and cruel emperor, a pleasure-driven man who ruled the world by whim and fear.

The young Nero, having been tutored by the servile philosopher and paedophile Seneca, was actually repulsed by the death penalty. But he resourcefully turned this weakness into strength: in 59 C.E. he had his mother stabbed to death for treason and his wife Octavia beheaded for adultery. He then had Octavia's head displayed for his mistress, Poppaea, whom years later he kicked to death when she was pregnant. The Senate made thank offerings to the gods for this restoration of public morality!

So, although there were many salacious stories to be reported, Dónal and his editor knew full well that such publication would result in their torture and death. In frustration, Dónal turned to the issue of Jewish Christian groups popping up throughout the empire for stories that might entertain his readers. He would return to the story of Nero in 64 C.E.

[Nero tried to pin the blame for the Great Fire of Rome in 64 C.E. on the city's small Christian community (regarded as a distinct, dissident group of Jews), and so, he burned many of them alive. Peter and Paul were said to have been martyred as a result. Political turmoil finally forced the troubled emperor to commit suicide. His last words were, *"What a showman the world is losing in me!"*]

A cache of ancient scrolls entitled *"Qui sunt isti Christiani usquam?"* has been discovered in the Liberties in Dublin. The scrolls were found by Professor Han van Meegeren who has translated them. They comprise a collection of various reports from a freelance investigative journalist named Dónal Questor that appeared in Rumor del Mundi in 54 C.E. and following years.
"Rumor del Mundi" was a weekly news publication with the highest circulation in Rome from circa 20 C.E. to 125 C.E. Its motto was: *"Shining a spotlight on what citizens need to know".*
Patois and dates have been amended to correlate with modern usage.

Táim Mealltóir.
Thomas Street,
Dublin.
May 2024.

65 C.E. Rumor Editor's note:
As readers will be aware there has been sporadic unrest in Judea over recent years. The principal instigators of these treasonable actions have been several organized groups such as the Sicarii and the Zealots. The most recent serious outbreak was instigated by brothers Simon and Jacob in 46 CE. Their revolt, which was concentrated in Galilee, began as a minor insurgency and when it climaxed in 48 CE it was quickly put down by the Roman authorities and both brothers were executed.

There is, however, another group which also originated in Jerusalem (or perhaps Galilee) and which has spread throughout the empire establishing a presence in many cities including Rome itself. It is particular sect of Jews who ally themselves with a little-known figure called *"Yeshua"*. For the benefit of our readers we will use the term, *"Jewish-Jews"* for members of the ancient religion of the inhabitants of the Province of

Judea. The sect we shall refer to as, "*Yeshua-Jews*" or "*Christians*". It is somewhat ominous that the Yeshua-Jews are sometimes referred to as "*Christians*" (a synonym for the phrase "*anointed ones*") and they talk of delivery and of a coming kingdom. Their founder was a man from a remote hamlet in Galilee who was executed some 32 years ago. The growth in the number of adherents and the ubiquity of their presence prompted this periodical to commission its most experienced reporter to investigate the matter.

Our reporter, Dónal Questor, is a refugee from Hibernia. He was forced to flee that country (an unruly barbaric island beyond Brittania and outside the empire) when he was sentenced to death by the Druids following a series of articles exposing underhand practices by them. Today, we reproduce below that reporter's articles. Dónal was utterly convinced that the Christians did not exist for religious reasons but consisted of zealous Jews and Jewish collaborators conspiring to overthrow the Roman Empire.

Following his death his executors released his personal diaries. We have included redacted excerpts from these diaries following each report. We believe these redacted excerpts and several of our interpolations will help the reader to have a better understanding of the progress of the investigation and the reporter's conclusions.

We accept no responsibility for the accuracy of alleged facts referred to in the reports or for the views of our reporter.

G. K. Chestertonius, editor. Martii 69 C.E.

I
Are Christians a threat? – the background.
Rome.
[A brief introduction to the break-away Jews]

At the Three Taverns on the Appian Way just south of Rome I met with a man named Paul who is on his way to face charges of being an agitator among the Jews and one of the ringleaders of the sect of Yeshua-Jews which broke off from mainstream Jewish Jews. He is quite an impressive fellow and has a pretty fantastic story to tell which is long on drama and hearsay but seems to be somewhat short on evidence. Anyway, it is a good story and readers can make up their own minds.

His story centres on a man named Yeshua, a Jew from an obscure village in the province occupied by the Jews to the east of Mare Nostrum. About 25 years ago this Yeshua was found guilty of some crimes (it is unclear what these were). He was condemned to death by the local Procurator and crucified. I've been able to verify this with an independent source (an historian by the name of Josephus) but it was some other things that Paul said that caused me some apprehension.

He says that on the third day after he died Yeshua came back to life and was seen by, talked with and shared meals with lots of people over the next forty days until he ascended up into the sky never to be seen again!

As you would expect I was highly sceptical. For example, did he actually die? It seems definite that his body disappeared from the tomb in which he was interred. But, was it simply removed by his followers? The Jewish hierarchy trenchantly allege that that was what happened. Was it Yeshua that was seen during the forty days, or a look-alike? There seems to be good reason to doubt the alleged rising from the dead since his closest and most ardent disciples did not recognize him when they first saw him subsequently. And then he just disappears. I have to say that I am thoroughly sceptical, but I'll dig a bit further into the matter since it seems to me that it may be a crafty subterfuge to camouflage their plan for subverting the empire.

Yeshua seems to have been a very peaceful man who went about Galilee for a very short time healing people and asking all to love one another and who eventually made his way to Jerusalem. Doesn't sound like a criminal type and I am puzzled as to what he might have done to merit the worst possible torture and death. It is apparent that he made a serious error in going to Jerusalem – the Jewish leaders there brooked no dissent.

Back to Paul. Paul said that this rising from the dead was possible because Yeshua was the Son of God! To get some idea of how outlandish all this is you have to understand that Paul doesn't believe in the gods as we do; he maintains that there is only one god and that that god is all-powerful.
Well, I warned him that if he starts to come up with that kind of stuff at his trial the Emperor is going to be mighty displeased with him and he should know what that would mean. Didn't seem to bother him! This Jew is quite audacious and fearless.

Yeshua was born some 58 years ago to a nondescript family and spent most of his life at home and unheard of outside his village until aged about 30. He was a builder by trade and the family lived in an obscure small town about four to five days' walk from Jerusalem. They were reasonably comfortable but there wouldn't have been any money for luxuries. Yeshua seems to have spent a lot of his spare time studying old Jewish traditions in a collection of writings they call the Tanakh.

Religion was the big preoccupation in that land at that time and had been for centuries. They make no differentiation between civil law and religious law. While all of the Jews have a lot in common there are many sects with niggling differences. One of the things that Jews have in common with one another is that it is second nature for them to niggle! An opinionated and contrary lot.
You have the High Priests who live off the fat of the land – they are very rich and comfortable and, while they are held in high esteem by everybody, they consider themselves to be superior to all the rest and avoid contact with the common people as much as they can. They control the only temple in the

province of Judea – the only Jewish temple in the world. It is situated on a hill in Jerusalem and it is a fantastic moneymaker.

One thing I can tell you about these priests is that they can put on wildly grandiose shows climaxing in a week-long one they call the Passover where more blood flows than you would see at any of our coliseums – although it is only the blood of animals instead of humans. The Jews come to this feast from all over the province and there would be hundreds of thousands of them in and around the city. I understand that it was during one of these feasts that they somehow managed to identify and capture Yeshua (they all look the same to us Romans!) and take him into custody. I sense that there is an intriguing story as to how the authorities found him and why they should be so bent on killing him and I will explore this matter in due course.

And then you have a small coterie of wealthy landowners. Then you have the Pharisees, Rabbis, Scribes, Essenes, Sadducees, and Zealots. And lastly you have the masses, a small number of whom are well off such as the tax collectors, although most of whom have just enough to get by and at the bottom rung you have the poor, sick and disabled who are automatically regarded as "*sinners*" and "*untouchables*" and are ritually unclean. Oddly, it was with these that Yeshua fraternized. So, I wonder, what harm could he have done? How could he have been even a minor threat or irritation to the powerful in the province?

As I said religion is the big deal and everybody has their own opinions on what is right and what is wrong and they have innumerable laws and commandments in relation to purification processes and a myriad of other religious observances. They seem to measure everything. They even have laws and rules about laws! Even though they have been conquered for umpteenth time they look down on us and everybody else and claim to be "*The Chosen People*". Chosen for what I don't know.

This Yeshua had a first cousin named John who had developed a reputation as a prophet. (For readers who are not familiar with what a prophet is they should think of an apocalyptic figure, a very independent guy who was thought to be able to read the signs of the times and warn as to what the future would hold). John was by all accounts a formidable figure who lived on his own in wilderness regions dressed in animal skins and living off whatever he could scavenge from the land.
He was a man who called a spade a spade, who called it as he saw it regardless of the consequences. An instance of this was in relation to the Jewish leader of Galilee, King Herod Antipater. On a visit to Rome Herod had fallen for his brother's wife, Herodias (and, can you believe it, she was also his (Herod's) niece). Following this he divorced his own wife, got Herodias to leave his brother and married her. This created a great scandal among the general populace as it was contrary to Jewish law. They frown on incest out there. It was also foolhardy since his first wife was the daughter of a powerful foreign king who then went to war with Herod and defeated him.

John was preaching a doctrine of repentance for sins (whatever they are) and baptizing (immersing in water) his followers as a sign of their change from a life of sin to one in keeping with Jewish religious teachings.
About the age of 30 Yeshua made his way to John and was baptized by him and then disappeared into the desert for a month or so.
While Yeshua was in the desert Herod had John arrested because he was afraid that he would incite the people to rebellion. His wife, Herodias, went one better: she got her daughter, Salome (see illustration on page 3) to dance for

Herod and his guests at his birthday party and seduced him into beheading John! You never knew where you stood with these people!

After returning from the desert Yeshua seems to have decided that he had a better message for his fellow Jews than the Pharisees, Sadducees etc. and he gathered several insignificant men around him and began wandering through Galilee, Samaria and Judea telling people about his worldview. He is accredited with healing blindness, leprosy, demonic possession and lameness and even with bringing people back to life from death. He became very popular with the masses and large crowds followed him everywhere he went.

The apparent miracles, however, were not what caused him to fall foul of the authorities, and in particular the High Priests in Jerusalem. The Pharisees and scribes were shocked to hear him telling people that their sins were forgiven and reported the matter to Jerusalem. The Herodians were also worried about him because he was talking about his coming kingdom. The Pharisees and scribes were scandalized to see him dining with tax collectors and sinners. Apparently, on one occasion, when dining with some Pharisees, scribes and lawyers on one occasion he turned on them and berated them calling them hypocrites and greedy and wicked so that they became very hostile towards him. My personal opinion is that they saw his popularity as a threat to the establishment particularly as he confounded their most erudite men in public discourses on several occasions.

I suppose that if he were doing all of this in Rome we would regard him as an irritating nuisance giving the plebs ideas above their station.

Paul has to move on to Rome now and has given me the address of the house in which he will be living. I'll catch up with him there in a week or so.

Dónal Questor.

Dónal's diary.

Maybe there isn't much of a story here. It seems to be some silly row between factions in the Jewish tribe. The Jews seem to be a race given to obsessing over minutiae. They have reams of rules about "clean" and "unclean" – so many that it is hard to see how any of them could be what they call "ritually clean". One thing I will say about the ones that I met is that they are hysterically obsessive about their opinions. Very difficult to have a rational discussion with them.

Paul is a Jew. But, while I detected some obsessiveness on his part he was quite open and receptive to questions. I have been pondering on the things that he told me. One thing that I don't understand is his assertion that faith in Yeshua is a gift from God. Why didn't his God make this "gift" to all of the Jews?

If there is such a God as he proclaims, and, if his God is all good why does not this God make a gift to all humans? I'm not aware of ever having been offered such a gift. Did I miss it?

I don't think so. This "gift" idea is a trick to cover up something illogical. I suppose that it is a matter of belief either way. We cannot sense this God. So, we either believe that he exists or we believe that he doesn't exist. So, have I a gift also? I believe God doesn't exist! That doesn't feel like a gift – it feels like common sense.

II
A meeting with Paul.

Rome.

I'm here in Rome with Paul, "*Paul of Tarsus*" as he likes to be known. Paul is staying in a modest villa here on the Via Piscium with a soldier on guard outside and he has many visitors. I want to find out more about Yeshua and how he got to be a criminal. Was he a murderer? Or a thief? Or a rebel – they call them Zealots or Sicarii. From what I have heard so far he seems to have been doing good deeds but aggravating the Jewish authorities along the way. At this time Paul has an old friend of his called Mark with him on a visit.

This fellow, Mark, is collecting material for a second book he is writing. During supper I asked him about his first book.
"*What is it about?*"
"*The good news of Yeshua, the Christ, the Messiah, the Son of God*" he replied.
"*Ma va a magna' er sapone, va.*" ["*Get out of here!*"]
Yes of course this startled me.
Doesn't he know that it is established that Caesar Augustus is called the "*son of god*" and is the great "*saviour*" of the whole earth through bringing "*peace*" (Pax Romana) to the empire, I asked him. This is what is heralded as "*good news*" I told him. If he puts something like that into circulation about this Yeshua he would quickly meet the same fate as Yeshua, I warned him. The 29 year-old emperor, Nero, was known for his intolerance of Christians.
Mark merely smiled.
"*Not only the Son of God*" intervened Paul, "*he also was and is God*".

I sniffed the wine to see if it contained opium or something like that.

No, it didn't.

"*Maniaci*" I thought.

Paul could see that I was quite upset and concerned about him. Paul and Mark went on to explain.

Over a millennium ago God used an ancestor of theirs named Moses to rescue their enslaved Jewish forefathers from Egypt and had given them the Land of Canaan, the present-day province of Judea. They claim that this had originally been owned by even older ancestors of theirs by the names of Abraham and Jacob/Israel.

Over the past 700 years they had been conquered and occupied many times starting with the Assyrians, followed by the Babylonians, Persians, Greeks and since about 120 years ago by Rome. Many Jews had been banished from their homeland and were scattered throughout the empire (all over the place like these Christians, I thought). But, based on a prophecy by Moses, they persist in the belief that a messiah from the line of David will deliver them from subjugation. About a thousand years ago King David had been a great warrior and so they expected their messiah to be a great prophet and warrior like Moses and David – there were many accounts in their sacred books of the Jews prevailing against vastly superior forces thanks to the intervention of God (but, as we know, papyrus never refused ink!).

Then, Paul began to read from chapter 53 of one of Isiah's books. It was strange stuff and I didn't really understand it. It was in the life and teachings of Yeshua that Isiah's vision has been clarified and consummated, he said. This messiah of theirs is not concerned about the kingdoms of this world – as the Son of God he brings near the Kingdom of God. He is a man of peace not war. He did not come to abolish the religion of the Jews – he came to fulfil it.

I didn't understand this, but, as a good reporter I am telling you what they said. It is a good cover story for their apparently non-seditious presence throughout the empire.

Paul and his followers have been banished by the Jews – the Jews want their political freedom now and they want a messiah who will bring that about. So, Paul and Mark have been travelling around other countries spreading what they insist on calling "*The Good News*" about Yeshua. Paul is now in hot water with the Roman establishment, but doesn't seem to be bothered by that. By now many of what the Jews call Gentiles share Paul's beliefs and there are ekklesiae in many cities, for example, Corinth, Philippi, Thessalonica, and even Rome itself. The whole thing with these Jewish-Jews and Yeshua-Jews seems very complicated and esoteric to me. I'm quite happy with our gods, Minerva, Venus, Apollo, etc., and, of course our beloved Caesar Augustus who made the city of Rome such a wonderful place for us Romans to live in. They give me whatever I need.

I can see why this peasant from Nazareth might be an irritant, but I don't understand why they would kill him in such a public manner. Surely, they could simply have thrown him in prison or put him on a galley ship or something like that – "*out of sight, out of mind*".

"*If they wanted to disappear him by killing him why not do so surreptitiously?*" I asked them.
"*They tried to kill him several times but he eluded them because it was not his time*", said Mark.
"*What do you mean?*" I asked.
"*He was always in charge. Several times he foretold that he would go to Jerusalem and be rejected by the Chief Priests and killed. He also reassured his followers that he would rise from the dead on the third day following this.*"

This startled me somewhat and I blurted out "*do you mean that he committed suicide?*"
Paul looked sympathetically at me. "*No. As he himself said:*

'I am the good shepherd. The good shepherd lays down his life for the sheep. And I lay down my life for the sheep. For this reason the Father loves me, because I lay down my life in order to take it up again. No one takes it from me, but I lay it down of my own accord.'

He was always in command of every situation in which he participated. Even when a large cohort of guards came to arrest him in the garden it was only when he permitted them to do so that they could lead him away".

I have to confess that I was a little stunned and lost for words at this stage. Yeshua sounded like one of our heroic gods. But this man was a vagrant who never held any position of consequence, never wrote any learned treatise (never wrote anything) and had a small ragtag following over a short period of time. He never achieved anything. Why is there so much fuss about him 30 years later?
Something is going on. There is more to this than meets the eye. It is apparent that this man, Yeshua, cannot be the inspiration for anything. He was not a hero.
I'm sensing the possibility of a big story here and shall investigate further.
More next week from your ever watchful reporter.

Dónal Questor.

Dónal's diary.

I'm getting an inkling of what the row between the Jewish/Jews and Yeshua/Jews is about. What seems to be the big deal concept for the Jews is their contention that there is only ONE God. But the Yeshua/Jews now say there is a second God – Yeshua. This Yeshua would seem to be a lesser god than the god of the Jews since he is claimed to be that god's son. But the Yeshua/Jews maintain that he is just as much God as his father. At the same time they will say that there is only one God. Reconcile that if you can!

I was tempted to ask them: "Aren't you also a son of God – after all, you tell me that he created you. So, aren't you as much God as Yeshua was? Or, should I say 'is'? Doesn't that mean that you think that we are all Gods? We Romans think that there are only a small number of gods and that seems much more reasonable to me." But, of course I didn't say any such thing. I am biding my time.

They talked about rising after dying and going to heaven to be happy for all eternity. But, didn't their Yeshua say: "Heaven and earth will pass away"? And, when they asked him when the end of earth would come he said: "...about that day no one knows, neither the angels of heaven, nor the Son, but only the Father." If they are both God (and the Jews maintain that there is only one God) how is it that the Son doesn't know as much as the Father? What we have are paradoxes.
I don't get it.

III.

The leaders and their stories.

Rome.
[Stories from Peter and Paul.]

We have received many communications from our readers concerning our coverage of this breakaway Jewish sect and I wish to reassure our readers that our loyalty and dedication to our glorious and beloved leader, the Divine Emperor Nero, is absolute and unswerving - long may he live and reign. Rome has never had much trouble with the Jewish people apart from minor disruptions in the Judaean province. However, we have observed that these dissident Jews (now going by the potentially pernicious name of "*Christians*", I have learnt) have spread to many regions in the empire in a very short space of time and are a cause of some unrest wherever they spring up. There is a possibility that they may be subversives and could grow in numbers and prevalence to constitute a danger to Rome.

Remember the revolt instigated in Roman Judea by the brothers Simon and Jacob several years ago. That was confined to the area of Galilee and was suppressed.

However, we are now seeing Christian sects sprouting up all over the world and their first loyalty seems to be to somebody other than our beloved Emperor. A worrying indication of where this may go can be appreciated from their refusal to recognize the gods and their claim that they have a superior god who is with them always. Also, they say, somewhat enigmatically, that "*the Kingdom of God is near*"!

And it should be noted that these cliques include non-ethnic Jews, (whom they call "*gentiles*") who are permitted to become members without having to become members of the Jewish religion. So, this is something new and international and the number of adherents is growing at an astonishing rate.

So far, we have not been able to establish where their inspiration comes from and it is unclear as to their motivation. It is known that they pool their resources and this is a further worrying sign.

As part of my independent and unbiased investigation of the matter I had the opportunity to talk with one of their leaders, a man called Peter, when I accompanied Mark on a visit to him. Mark was looking for some material from an eye witness for the second book he is writing. It concerns the alleged resurrection of Yeshua and his post-resurrection activities. (Note: I intend to get access to his draft as soon as I can).

This Peter is also under house arrest. At first sight he seems somewhat frail. I had a feeling that he didn't want to meet with me but after a chat with Mark some of his followers led him to me and I could see that he was blind (Imagine that: a blind eyewitness!). But when he began to speak of his lord and master (Yeshua) he was transformed and became euphoric and effusive. He used expressions such as "*Messiah*" and "*Son of the living God*". I pointed out to him that Caesar was a son of god and asked if Yeshua and he were brothers. Whereupon he claimed that Yeshua was God. I have to say that I blinked. I asked him how he knew this and he said that Yeshua told him that it was revealed to him, Peter, by Yeshua's Father in heaven!

You can see, dear reader, that he is terribly confused. He thinks that Yeshua is God plus the son of God because Yeshua told him that God had let him know this. One doesn't have to be a philosopher to see the contradictions inherent in this. I thought to myself: "*whatever makes you happy*" and mentally rolled my eyes.

That God stuff doesn't seem to be a particular problem for us. The Jews have been going on about it for ages. It is this reference to a "*Messiah*" that worries me. "*Messiah*" is a

Hebrew word. It means an anointed one, the same as the Greek word "*Christ*". And who gets anointed? A person who is just about to become king. In this sense Moses was a messiah. And, what is Moses famous for? For delivering the Jewish people out of Egypt and from under the rule of the Pharaohs. So, if Yeshua is to deliver his people from under Roman rule, where are they to go? There isn't anywhere outside the empire that would tolerate them. It therefore seems that they would have to depose our beloved Emperor and the Senate and replace them with their leaders and replace our rules with theirs. This would be catastrophic. An example of some of their rules are:

- Forgive your enemies – even *love* your enemies;
- Forgive your enemy seventy-seven times;
- It is good to be poor!;
- It is very good to be meek;
- You are blessed when you are persecuted;
- If anyone slaps you on the right cheek, turn to them the other cheek also;
- whoever wants to sue you and take your coat, leave for him also your cloak.

And so on and on. You can see how misguided these people are and how steeped they are in some kind of sloppy sentimental notion of maudlin love.

There was one follower of Yeshua who eventually saw through his illogical talk and magic tricks. His name was Judas. He was getting fed up with all the talk which was getting nowhere and with no action. When he saw Yeshua allow some woman to smear his feet (his feet!) by wasting an extremely expensive lotion doing so, he had enough. How could a man such as this possibly consider he could "*deliver*" his people? So, Judas made a deal with the head religious leaders. In return for a useful amount of money he would point Yeshua out to them so that they could take him into custody. He did this and Yeshua was arrested. Judas died shortly afterwards.

I found it hard to make out what kind of person Peter was. Sometimes he seems simple and then he comes out with some highly complex and mystical utterances. He certainly held me spellbound when I asked him how he came to be a follower of Yeshua.

"I was introduced to him by my brother, Andrew, who announced to me 'We have found the Messiah'. Later, Yeshua looked at me and said 'Follow me' and I did. I don't know why. I left everything and went everywhere with him until his death. I fell in love with him. It wasn't an earthly love, it was a great feeling of trust and well-being in his company. I could see that he was a good man – everything he did was loving and caring for others. And he had wonderful sayings, many of which I didn't understand, and a beautiful outlook on life. Then, one day, I knew that he was God and the Messiah spoken of in Sacred Scripture. But then I also found that I didn't know much about the nature of God. But, then again, I was learning, learning from him. Can you imagine how fulfilling it was to learn about God from God? And yet, when it came to the moment of crisis, the moment of his trial and crucifixion I deserted him – I denied being his follower.
Oh, the intense agony of those days"

Tears were running down his cheeks as he recounted this.

"And then the...the...the...miracle of miracles. He had, by his own divine power, risen from being dead as he had told us several times he would. He was alive again. He, being God and all-powerful, had simply become alive again and, although the physicality of his body was enhanced in some mystical manner, he was the same Yeshua that I had loved and I still did and I still do. He remained with us for about six weeks sharing meals and thoughts. Then, instructing us to tell all peoples about him and his message of mercy and forgiveness he disappeared

before our eyes fulfilling what he had previously said to Mary: 'Go instead to my brothers and tell them, 'I am ascending to my Father and your Father, to my God and your God'."

I asked him if that was when he and his companions began to spread the word about Yeshua.

"No. Once he had gone we were again very scared. The leaders of the Jews were in a rage because so many ordinary people were saying that Yeshua had risen from the dead and they were determined to stomp out those who expressed this view. And they had goaded the Romans into helping them in putting an end to it. We went back into a room in the city as he had commanded us and stayed there. We felt powerless without him and we were afraid. He had told us that we would receive power from a holy spirit but we didn't know what that meant."

I have to say that I was at a loss as to what all the fuss was about. An uneducated peasant from a remote insignificant village is supposed to deliver his people from the might of the Roman empire, and, what has he done? He is not of noble stock, has no education, no army or weapons, and a handful of riffraff followers. The puzzling thing is that, given this, why should the Jewish authorities have been in such apprehension of him as to coerce the Roman authorities into killing him. And, not only him I have heard stories of how they hounded and killed his followers. In fact, I have heard it said that Paul was once a leading crusader in this pogrom.
Peter was exhausted by now and so we parted as his friends led him off to his room.

At supper that night Paul was holding forth as usual. I couldn't understand what he was talking about. For example, (and I wrote this bit down as he talked): *"There is neither Jew nor*

Gentile, neither slave nor free, nor is there male and female, for you are all one in Christ Yeshua". Doesn't make any sense, does it? I mean, everywhere you look there are Jews and Gentiles and slaves. So, your intrepid and fearless reporter interrupted him saying,
"I have been given to understand that you didn't always think this way. Is that correct?"
An uneasy hush fell over the room. Paul seemed to shrink and crumble before our eyes. I felt a sense of misgiving and that I should have kept my big mouth shut – after all, I was a guest in his house. Paul rallied quickly. He turned his piercing compassionate eyes on mine mesmerizing me as he spoke.

"Alas, yes. You are correct. I was a Pharisee and the son of a Pharisee and I was trained in the Law and the Prophets by the great Gamaliel. I was obsessively impassioned with the word of God as revealed to us in the Scriptures. I was determined to eradicate what I saw as apostates and restore the Tradition for all. So, yes, I persecuted the followers of Yeshua."
There was a pause and I asked *"so what happened to make you change your mind?"*
"He met Yeshua" interjected Mark.
I sniffed, *"But I thought you said that, following his rising from death, Yeshua had gone from this world"* I challenged.
Silence.
Paul spoke again.
"I had been commissioned by the High Priest to go to Damascus and bring back as prisoners the followers of Yeshua who were living there.

> Note for our readers: it is a journey of 300 miles from Jerusalem to Damascus and would take about a fortnight on foot and about a week on horseback.

I was on my way when, suddenly, there was a tremendous flash of light from the sky and it was all around me. I was blinded and fell to the ground. Then I and all of the men travelling with me heard a voice saying: 'Saul, Saul, why do you persecute me?' I noticed that the voice said 'me' and not 'us'. So, I asked, 'Who are you, Lord?'".

"Hold on" I interrupted, "Your name is 'Paul', not 'Saul'"

"At that time it was 'Saul' but the old Saul has changed more radically than his name."

"Oh!"

He went on, "The answer to my question completely astonished me. The voice said...",

and here Paul paused and looked penetratingly at me,

"I am Yeshua, whom you are persecuting. But get up and enter the city, and you will be told what you are to do."

There was a fairly long period of silence following this. I have to admit that I couldn't get my mind around what I was being told. It was irrational, if not actually insane. One thing for sure is that this Yeshua had a very strong personality and charisma. But he failed to convince the religious establishment of anything and the civil establishment couldn't have cared less about him.

He wandered about the country undermining the traditions, and then he died, and then he became alive again for a short while after which he disappeared and then, yet again, he (or his voice) is talking with Saul. What were these people up to? I reverted to the old question: *Cui bono?* – who profits? I don't get it. They have had nothing but trouble and strife from the religious and civil authorities. And none of them seems to have any money or treasure or land. Yet, they seem to be a happy and contented lot. None of this makes any sense.

Yet!

Something is going on and rest assured, dear readers, that your resolutely determined reporter who is interested only in the truth will ferret out and reveal what it is.

Might they be fifth columnists for a foreign kingdom?

I slept somewhat uneasily that night.

I decided that I would visit Jerusalem, the source of this unrest, on the following day.

      Dónal Questor.

Dónal's diary.
There is no doubt that this Yeshua was a very disruptive fellow. At the same time he seems to have done a lot of healing and to have been very popular with the hoi polio. And he doesn't seem to have said anything against Rome – in fact quite the opposite: he encouraged the Jews to pay their taxes. He even dined with tax collectors and had one of them as a close follower. It seems that it was only the Jewish establishment that was averse to him. Could he have been supporting Rome against the Jews, I wondered?

All this talk about it being okay to be poor and meek and turn the other cheek seems to indicate that. That attitude in our colonies would have suited us very well.

Maybe he is a god like Mars and in opposition to the God of the Jews and on the side of Rome. But, that seems unlikely since we had him executed. Although the Jews wanted rid of him as well.

I'm beginning to wonder if this Christian stuff is all down to Paul. He is the fellow who seems to have done most to spread news and stories about Yeshua outside Judea. Yeshua's chosen followers have stayed in Jerusalem and only dealt with fellow Jews. It is Paul who has been travelling all over the place and bringing what he calls "the Good News" to non-Jews. Setting up cults in various cities by watering down the Jewish Law and practices to suit the pagans. Telling them that, although Yeshua was a Jew, they needn't be circumcised, or follow the innumerable rules tabulated in the Jews' sacred books. So, they could get to be special and enjoy heavenly bliss for eternity after they died without the hassle the Jews insisted on. The new and superior "chosen" people!
I don't yet know exactly what it is, but, this Paul fellow is up to something.

The Judean background

Nazareth
[A backwater.]

On the way to Jerusalem, I stopped off in Nazareth for a day. The word was that this is where Yeshua came from. Nazareth is set in a small basin surrounded by hills and is not very accessible. It has a water supply from a well, and there is some limited terraced agriculture, as well as pasture fields. But, since the town isn't located on or near a travel route, people don't go to or through Nazareth unless they specifically want to go there.

The Nazareans have underground pits for wine production and storage. Interestingly I discovered that they have dug below the pits, down to a second level, deeper down, and a third level, and often there are underground passages leading from one to another. This is so that in the times of danger or when people want to hide things, they are able to do so.

For instance, it is believed that the pits have been used to hide possessions and from the eyes of the Roman authorities.

Over fifty years ago Yeshua's father, Joseph, had come there from Egypt. He had fled to Egypt from Judea to escape a massacre of babies by King Herod who was paranoically afraid that one of the babies might be a potential king in the line of the House of David.

It is a small backward hamlet inhabited by somewhat primitive and unsophisticated people living a humdrum existence. It could not be a seedbed for resistance to Rome. Indeed, one wonders if anything good could come out of Nazareth. In a word, it is boring and I was glad to move on.

Jerusalem
[An obnoxious priest.]

Jerusalem is a very different story.

From a distance the Temple dominates the hilltop. It is a spectacularly impressive building ranking with any we have in our capitol city.

The Jews say that their god resides there in what they call "*The Holy of Holies*".
But there is a thriving bustling marketplace inside and outside the walls. I sat in the shade for a while watching the hagglings and the comings and goings. Nowhere in the empire have I seen

so effective an endeavour for extracting the maximum money possible from visitors. It has a bank to mind the monies of the wealthy Jews. And activities seem to go on all through the year reaching peaks during celebrations like the Passover when they remember their delivery from Egypt.

I couldn't get an interview with the High Priest (who is the supreme religious authority for the Jews) but managed to meet with a priest by the name of Joseph ben Gurion. When I asked him about the man who died about 25 years ago and his followers, he became somewhat apoplectic. Stripped of its invective and my interlocutions, the following is the gist of what he told me.

"That person was nothing but a rabble rouser. He misled many of our ignorant peasants with misinterpretations of Scripture. We know, for instance, that his own family and kinsfolk from his village, Nazareth, wanted nothing to do with him – indeed they thought that he was mad. And they were right. He was in league with Beelzebub and he even told his followers that they should eat his body and drink his blood. Furthermore, and most appallingly he claimed to be YHWH and to be able to forgive sins. And, of course the gullible people to whom he appealed were of the lowest class, tax collectors, the unclean, prostitutes, beggars and so on.
Eventually, and in order to protect our fellow Jews, we managed to capture him. We gave him a fair trial and he was found guilty of blasphemy. The punishment for blasphemy in Jewish law is death by stoning. But, under Roman Law, we were not permitted to carry out a punishment of death. So, in keeping with the law we brought him before the Governor, who at that time was Pontius Pilate. The governor gave him a fair hearing and, although Pilate dithered somewhat in his efforts to be seen to be fair and give the miscreant every chance to save himself, Pilate eventually ordered his execution by

crucifixion at the behest of the outraged faithful – the sentence was unanimous. He was crucified, died and was entombed.

However, he had deeply infected his followers with his evil superstitions and, of course Beelzebub had also possessed them, so that, some days later, they stole his body from the tomb and claimed that he had risen to life again. Well, as you know: when you die, you die. And you remain dead forever. Nobody has ever died and come to life again."

"*What about Lazarus?*" I had the temerity to suggest.

Another hysterical eruption.

"*That was just superstitious nonsense. It is clear that he wasn't dead, but rather, that he was mistakenly entombed. One notices that the Nazarene didn't say 'Arise from the dead, Lazarus', he said 'Lazarus, come forth'*".

"*Very well*" I said, "*but what about his ongoing popularity and the growing numbers of people following him?*" I asked.

"*Are you also one of his followers?*" he snarled at me.

I hastily assured him that I most assuredly was not – "*My gods are our Roman gods. I do not believe in any life after death. 'Eat, drink and be merry today, for tomorrow we die' is my motto*".

Although he looked at me with what I could only take to be an expression of disdain he also seemed somewhat mollified.

"*His followers are mostly barbarians and gentiles of lowly status*", he continued. "*The Temple remains the home of YHWH on this earth and, one day, all will return to worship here in the Temple as Ezekiel has foretold*".

Turning on his heel he swept out of the room followed by his flunkies and that was the last I saw of him or heard from him.

I need to do some thinking and some more investigation. There is something that I am not seeing.

We need to remember that the Jewish people have been around for more than twelve hundred years, which is a fair bit longer than Rome. They have developed a sophisticated system of laws and traditions. There are about seven to eight million of them scattered through the empire. The upper classes are highly educated. Their main claim is that there is only one God who is the creator of the world and who is all powerful and that this god has chosen the Jewish race as his people in preference to all other nations. I can attest that they consider themselves as vastly superior to all other peoples. Even the many coteries of them scattered through the empire keep to themselves observing the Jewish law and rituals and dealing with the locals mainly in matters of trade and commerce.

The principal belief of these traditional Jews and the breakaway sect of Christians is that there is only one God. They think that this god is all-powerful and absolutely perfect and that he created the world and humans.
What an absurd fantasy. All one has to do is look around at the world with its diseases, floods, deserts, wild animals, volcanoes, and so on. Not to mention the evil in humans who kill and rape and steal and war and lie. Why would a god who could do anything he wished make such a world or people? It wouldn't make any sense unless he was arbitrarily malicious and uncaring of his own creation. But they say he is good and loving. It is not hard to see the incongruity in their fundamental premise. Our conviction that there many and varied gods toying with us from time to time makes much more sense.
One wonders, therefore, why they should be so upset by an uneducated yokel who wandered around the country for a couple of years accompanied by an insignificant number of unarmed kinsfolk? After all, Rome never had the slightest interest in him although it has been necessary every now and then to chastise some of his followers for failure to pay due homage to the emperor.

There is more to this sect than meets the eye, and, I am determined to find out what it is even if it is some kind of contagious mental disease.

Dónal Questor

Dónal's diary.

Maybe this whole upheaval is about tax fraud. I have observed that most Jews live in very poor conditions while the hierarchy who are in a minority have opulent lifestyles which rival any in Rome. In contrast the ordinary Jews are impoverished by the amounts taken from them in taxes.

Perhaps a tax audit of the controllers of the Temple is required. Is this what might have enraged them when Yeshua said to them, "render unto Caesar what is Caesar's"? And, apparently he was hanging around the temple a lot and watching the business being done – a lot more business than praying it seems.

And he predicted that the Temple would be torn down. By whom? By the legions acting for the Roman tax collectors searching for hidden monies? Is this "corban" thing whereby if you pledge your money to God it can't be used for anything else a justification for not paying taxes?

Suppose an audit resulted in bankruptcy of the establishment and imprisonment (or worse!) of the priests. The fear of such a calamity would surely provoke the priests to seek to eradicate the potential risk – "whatever it takes" one might say.

V
A Pharisee's observations.
Jerusalem.
[One Jew's dilemma.]

This morning I saw a Pharisee standing in the Court of the Gentiles at the periphery of the Temple. I sensed that he was somewhat ill at ease. He might have some insights into these Christians and so I approached him.
"*Ave, Pharisee.*"
"*Ave*".
"*Are you a follower of Yeshua?*" I asked him.
He looked around somewhat furtively and responded: "*Are you?*"
"*No. I am a reporter with Rumor del Mundi. I am trying to find out the reasons for which these sects exist.*"
"*Oh. Well, they believe that Yeshua is the long-awaited Messiah.*"
"*And, do you believe that he is?*"
"*Well, he seems to have been a very good man who did many extraordinary things and uttered many wise sayings. He exorcised many demons. He sided with the poor and oppressed. He confounded the scribes and lawyers with his understanding of The Law and the Prophets. He never sought worldly goods or fame or renown for himself.*"
"*But he was convicted as a criminal and put to death by crucifixion, wasn't he? So, is that why you are not a follower?* I asked him.
"*No.*"
"*What, then?*"
"*The great revelation made to our ancestors was that there is only one God who is almighty and by whom all persons and things are created and who holds all in the palm of his hand. It was he, through the prophet Moses, who revealed to us the Law showing us what is right and what is wrong and how we should*

live our lives. We may not have strange gods before him nor take his name in vain."

"Well, what has that to do with Yeshua?"

"Yeshua claimed to be God or the Son of God, as if such a thing were possible. But there is only one God."

I sighed. Here was this introvertive reductionist conception again.

"What's the problem with that? Doesn't Caesar claim to be a god? Why couldn't this Yeshua be a god. What harm could it do if he was?"

"A man who by his very nature is finite could not be God who by His very nature is beyond finite, who is non-finite, who is spirit and non-material. It is a contradiction in terms" yelped my new acquaintance. He was getting somewhat agitated.

"Pax, pax. What is your name?"

"Theophilous."

"Well, Theo...may I call you Theo? My name is Dónal. What you call a contradiction in terms becomes so because you introduce this conception of there being only one god. Nobody believes that there are no gods, but most believe there are many gods. Very few believe that there is only one God, but, again, many believe there are many gods. So, which is more likely? One God or many gods?"

"I believe that there is only one being who is God" replied Theo, "I cannot accept that the world has always existed. It had to start at the first moment of time. If the existence of the world was with no beginning, then, since we cannot see back to a beginning, one could never reach the present moment. Therefore, there must be a being who is outside time and space who, in itself, had no beginning and who made space for the world to exist in and who made the world which lies timebound in that space. How could such a being be encompassed in a human? How could a human be God?"

He paused for breath. Just as well because I wasn't following him. He had obviously thought about the matter.

"So, you think that he was an imposter?" I asked.

"No, no. that is too harsh. As far as I can gather, he was very wise and kind and performed many good works. I am puzzled, though. If he had simply claimed to be our long awaited Messiah I might have aligned myself with him. I find myself in sympathy with most of what he said. But, to accept that he could be a son of God is a step too far. If he had claimed to be God in human form I might have been able to give credence to such a claim. I say 'might' because of the catastrophic end to which he came – that could not happen to God, or, to a human-like representation of God."

"But, don't the Christians say that he came back to life?" I said in an effort to provoke him.

"They do indeed. But there is no evidence for that other than the words of some uneducated peasants and women. That is not enough for me."

"Well, some Christians I have met told me that belief in him is a gift" I said hoping to urge him on.

He looked at me wistfully. *"Then I have not received any such gift. And now, I must take your leave as it is time for prayer".* He turned on his heel and disappeared into the Temple.

So much for the idea of a gift, I thought. Here was a man who had led a good life earnestly in keeping with the Law and the Prophets; one who had given serious thought to the words and deeds of Yeshua. Why wouldn't such a one receive the "gift" of belief if there were a God who was good?

Dónal Questor

<u>Dónal's diary.</u>
If a good living Pharisee who has studied the so-called Sacred Books doesn't understand these Christians, how can we? Probably because they are not about religion but some conspiracy to escape Roman rule – to be "delivered from evil" as their ancestors were by Moses, "evil" being the coded word for Rome.

Publishers' note.

The problem that arose was clear: how could Christ be both divine and human, since the two are so immeasurably distinct? Humans are fallible in every way, God is perfect in every way: omnipotent, infallible, omnipresent, omniscient, eternal. The gap seems unbridgeable. Could Christ be partly divine and partly human? Is that even possible? But if he was fully human, how could he be at all divine, and if he was fully divine, how could he be at all human? This question provides a good insight into the nature of theology. That Christ was both human and divine has become a matter of Christian belief. The problem was how to explain that belief, and that is what theology strives to do. To cite the classic definition given by the medieval theologian Anselm of Canterbury, theology is faith seeking understanding; that is, the theologian starts from her or his personal faith and the faith of the community, and tries to understand and explain that faith as well as she or he can. Early Christian theologians who accepted Christ's humanity and divinity sought a way to reconcile the two.

Kelly, Joseph F. The Origins of Christmas.
See Appendix on Nicene Creed as amended by Council of Constantinople.

VI.

A meal with some Christians.
Jerusalem.
[Could this be all they do?]

Yesterday I learnt more about this eccentric cult of breakaway Jews. They form themselves into cells, each comprising up to fifty adherents. The groups are heterogeneous, comprising any age or sex, Romans, Jews, freemen, slaves, nobility and commoners. And, there is a large number of them scattered through the cities and towns of the Empire. There doesn't seem to be a central leader although they seem to defer to Peter and there are many itinerant emissaries like Paul who visit them from time to time.
It is difficult to know what it is that keeps them together. They say that they are followers of that man Yeshua who died some 25 years ago, but I can't see that he ever achieved anything whatsoever. And, although they call him the great deliverer, I can't fathom what it is from which he was supposed to have delivered them. Nothing has changed. Life goes on as it was before he appeared for a few years – apart from the cliques set up after his death.

I was invited to supper in one of their houses. Of course, I accepted this invitation in the hope that someone might drop a clue as to what they hope to achieve. It took me a while to discover that the leader of the group was a middle-aged Nubian. Yes, a Nubian! His name was Ameny and they said that he was a prophet. The meal consisted of rather humble fare. The conversation was about the various exploits of Yeshua and the stories that he had told. They really loved these stories although they must have heard them countless times. The meeting culminated in talk about the meal he shared with his followers on the night before he was executed. An expectant hush fell on the diners as Ameny recalled his words in sharing bread and wine.

"Our Lord said, 'I have eagerly desired to eat this Passover with you before I suffer', and we now eagerly desire to eat this eucharistic bread and drink this eucharistic wine with him, for, as he said 'this is my body which is given you for you'"

He then said something similar over his wine and passed some bread and his goblet of wine to the participants, including yours truly. After eating and drinking there was silence for a while followed by a hymn, and then everybody departed for their homes.

There have been rumours that these gatherings are occasions of cannibalism and orgy. Let me assure readers that there was not anything remotely like such behaviour at this gathering. Of course, they would have been conscious of my presence and my reputation for unearthing the truth and exposing miscreants. There were, however, some things that have been rattling around in my mind. They opened proceedings with a prayer said to have been taught to them by Yeshua. In this they asked for their god's kingdom to come – and I wondered if this might be a veiled threat to overthrow Roman rule. Also, they asked for their god's will to be done – his laws instead of those of the Emperor and the Senate? Then in closing they asked to be delivered from evil. What "*evil*"? Is this a coded word for Rome?

There is something going on; something far-reaching; something subtle. And the number involved is growing. I ask myself: which would I rather face – an army of ten thousand – or an apparently peaceful mob of five million? I went to sleep remembering Cato's famous phrase;

"*Carthāgō dēlenda est*".

Should we now be saying:

"*Christianitas dēlenda est*".

Dónal Questor

Dónal's diary.

While I need to keep an open mind, those attending tonight's dinner all seemed to be peace loving and gentle. Of course, they had a Roman citizen as a guest and that would have influenced their behaviour. There was no talk or hint of any action against the Jewish establishment or against Rome.

But, Amadan wrote that "there is an ancient doctrine which has existed from the beginning, which has always been maintained by the wisest nations and cities and wise men". He blames Moses for the corruption of the ancient religions: "the goatherds and shepherds who followed Moses as their leader were deluded by clumsy deceits into thinking that there was only one God, and, without any rational cause these goatherds and shepherds abandoned the worship of many gods"

However, Amadan's harshest criticism was reserved for Christians, who "wall themselves off and break away from the rest of mankind".

Amadan wants them to be good citizens, to retain their own belief but worship the emperors and join their fellow citizens in defending the empire. This appeal on behalf of unity and mutual toleration nevertheless centres on submission to the state and military service. One of Amadan's bitterest complaints is that Christians refused to cooperate with civil society and held local customs and the ancient religions in contempt.

Amadan warned that the Christians would subvert the traditions and beliefs of the empire if they were not soon stopped.

Maybe he is correct – they are certainly proliferating throughout the empire.

Are they simply biding their time?

Or, am I missing something?

VII.

Where the controversy began and a liberated female.
Capernaum.
[The original group.]

Today I headed up to Capernaum which seems to have been the home base of Yeshua and his closest followers. Capernaum is a fishing village that was established during the time of the Hasmoneans. It is located on the northern shore of the Sea of Galilee and has a population of about 1,500. According to Ameny, Yeshua lived in Nazareth and left it at the age of 30 years. He then lived in Capernaum, the town to which he would return after his peregrinations around Galilee, nearby gentile lands and visits to Jerusalem.

I met with a man named Simon who had come from Cyrene in Libya and settled in Capernaum following a memorable encounter with Yeshua. He told me that a man called Matthew had been the Tax Collector in the town and became one of Yeshua's first followers as did a man by the name of Phillip who introduced Nathaniel to the group. Before that, the first followers came from the town of Bethsaida, about three miles away. They were the two brothers Andrew and Simon Peter (who is currently in Rome), the two brothers James and John and the man called Nathaniel.
Prior to following Yeshua, they had encountered a man called John who lived in Bethany beyond the Jordan river, just North of the Dead Sea (see my article on John). John was an awe-inspiring figure and had told them that coming after him was a mightier person who would baptize them, not just with water, but with the Holy Spirit whatever that meant. Well, I thought, that should have been a lesson for them, because as I recall it,

that man was summarily executed by King Herod for insulting his wife, Herodias.

Simon told me there were 12 close followers known to all as the "*apostles*" which comes from a Greek word meaning "*persons sent*". They travelled with Yeshua on all of his journeys. It seems to me that Yeshua was putting together an inner circle to whom he was giving secret instructions on how to achieve their aims following his possible death before he could achieve these results. (It is reported that he used to meet with them after talking to the general populace to explain to them what he meant – for example the story of Lazarus and the rich man). What aims? Could it be that the "*good news*" for the gentiles is telling them that there is a network of maverick Jews and gentiles throughout the Empire who would assist them in **delivering** them from their Roman masters. There are about 50 countries in our empire, Gauls, Spanish, English, Egyptian, Greek, Turkish and so on. The strategy of Julius Caesar was to "*divide and conquer*". Could the strategy of these mavericks be to "*collaborate and repulse*"? We don't have any idea how numerous these mavericks have become.

Magdala.
[Stranger and stranger.]

In the afternoon I sailed down to Magdala Nunayya. I had heard that visiting there at this time was a woman by the name of Mary who had been a close follower and supporter of Yeshua. I found her washing clothes with other women on the bank of a small stream. It may seem a little uncanny, but from a distance I knew which of the women was Mary and felt that she sensed my approach. As I reached her, she turned around. "*Shalom*" she greeted me, and having become accustomed to some of their ways, I responded "*Aleichem shalom*". She smiled.
"*What is it that you seek?*" she asked. Direct, wasn't she?

Well, I was not about to let her set the agenda and so I launched straight in with,

"*We are trying to find out what the followers of Yeshua are about. And what they mean when they talk about 'good news' and 'deliverance'. And why they have abandoned the ways of orthodox Jews. What is your big secret?*"

"*There are no secrets. We have not abandoned the Law of the Jews. In fact, it is the opposite. All is revealed.*"

"*Well, it hasn't been revealed to me. What are you trying to achieve?*"

There was a pause for about a minute, and then she said,

"*The Word was made flesh and dwelt among us*".

This was gibberish to me. I hadn't a clue as to what it was supposed to mean. I began to wonder if she was playing some kind of game with me.

"*You are babbling and avoiding the question. What is this 'word'?*"

"*Yeshua is the Word and the Word is God who created this universe and everything in it. And, in our time, the Word became a man and lived with us. He taught us the way to live. He opened our eyes to the truth that we might have life in him. He is the Way, the Truth and the Life.*"

What was she talking about, I wondered.

"*But he has been dead for over 25 years*", I interjected.

"*He rose from the dead. He is alive and lives with us until the end of time.*"

As you can see, dear readers, the poor woman is quite demented, possibly having hallucinations. If, as Peter and Paul had said, he ascended into the sky, how could he be living with them? I decided to humour her and so I asked her,

"*What has he done for you?*"

"*He taught me to dance*".

I do not exaggerate – that's what the poor thing said to me. I played along.

"He taught you to dance?" said I in a somewhat high-pitched voice.

"Yes. The Law and the Prophets taught me the steps or rules of various dances. I learnt them with my head. They made sense. But they were difficult to carry out and I always felt I was going against the grain. And there were many times when I couldn't be bothered to follow those steps. You see, the steps were in my head. So, I did my own thing. I led a dissolute life. Then I met him."

"Who?" I asked, although I could guess the answer.

"Yeshua".

"And what happened?" I asked.

"The Holy Ghost came down upon me. He now dwells in my heart."

"What on Earth are you babbling about?" I asked in exasperation.

"It was as though a light shone. The music of love filled my heart and I knew Truth. I knew gratitude. I knew trust. I knew Love. Now the steps are in my heart. Now I can dance to the tune and rhythm of a heart filled with a trusting love and with no need to think of any rules or any steps. I am free. It is so liberating that the steps are in my heart, a heart now filled with the music of love. The rules are no longer needed because I am in harmony with God. Even now, as I stand talking with you, I am dancing in my heart to the music in my heart. And I ask you to join with us in the dance. Can't you hear it?"

Somewhat bewildered I assured her that I couldn't hear.

She smiled. *"Ask, and it will be given you; seek, and you will find; knock, and it will be opened to you. For everyone who asks receives, and he who seeks finds, and to him who knocks it will be opened'.*

Totally and completely off her head, I thought. But, dangerous? I don't know.

"What about the male followers of Yeshua?" I asked.

"What about them?".

"*Do they also dance?*" I asked, somewhat tickled at my pun.
"*We are all part of the great agapé with Yeshua*" she replied.
Too much. I thanked Mary for her time and headed back. I decided that I needed to get more information from Paul and Mark and so next day I headed back to Rome.

Dónal Questor

<u>Dónal's diary.</u>
I am still somewhat shaken following my meeting with that woman. There was something other-worldly about her. While she was gracious and charming and although I could not understand most of what she said I was shaken. I don't know why. Was she necromantic, I wondered? Might she be an agent of Orcus? And, what on earth is an "agapé"?
Are all of these Christians deranged?
Are they on some kind of drugs?
Is "gift" a pseudonym for drugs?
Or, am I missing something?
I have to admit that more and more there is something that I don't get. I hope it doesn't turn out to be something as banal and trite as cannabis.

VIII.

A thorn in the side of the establishment.
Rome.
[Yeshua, a thorn in the side of the establishment.]

Mark is a busy man. When he is not running errands for Peter and Paul he spends his time questioning visiting Christians and finishing his second book (his first gospel was written over fifteen years ago). I pinned him down for a few moments. I told him that I had met with several groups of Christians and that overall, they seemed to be quite harmless. Why, I wanted to know, were they so much hated and persecuted by the Temple Jews. By way of answer busy Mark showed me a passage from his first book which had been written with non-Jews in mind. He had obtained the account from a former Pharisee by the name of Joseph of Arimithea. I reproduce it below:

The Pharisees and Sadducees and scribes were continually posing crafty questions to Yeshua with a view to finding him in error. One day the chief priests, the scribes, and the elders came upon Yeshua in the Temple and again they tried to wrongfoot him. So, he then told them the following story:

A man planted a vineyard, put a fence around it, dug a pit for the wine press, and built a watch-tower; then he leased it to tenants and went to another country.

When the season came, he sent a slave to the tenants to collect from them his share of the produce of the vineyard. But they seized him, and beat him, and sent him away empty-handed.

And again, he sent another slave to them; this one they beat over the head and insulted.

Then he sent another, and that one they killed. And so it was with many others; some they beat, and others they killed.

He had still one other, a beloved son.

Finally, he sent him to them, saying, "They will respect my son." But those tenants said to one another, "This is the heir; come, let us kill him, and the inheritance will be ours." So, they seized him, killed him, and threw him out of the vineyard. What then will the owner of the vineyard do? He will come and destroy the tenants and give the vineyard to others.

They realized that he had told this story against them. They were enraged and wanted to arrest him, but they feared the crowd. So, they left him and went away until there would be a more opportune time.

I was beginning to understand why the leaders of the Jews hated this man so much. Their main claim to greatness was that they were the chosen people, chosen by their god in preference to all the other nations in the world. This peasant comes along and implies that he is their deliverer, but he doesn't correspond with their expectation of a great warrior like David. He tells them that they will no longer be special. In fact, this man's god will destroy them.
I have heard it said that it was these head men of the Jews who brought Yeshua to court and found him guilty of something – something so terrible that it justified his death. Well, I hadn't heard of anything being done by him that would justify such a verdict – in fact, quite the opposite. Apart from what he

may have said he seemed to be a great healer. He was setting the ordinary people free. Free from their misdeeds, free from physical maladies and free from obsessive scrupulousness. My curiosity was piqued. Could there have been an egregious miscarriage of justice, I wondered? Or, was he a wolf in sheep's clothing? As it happened one of the original followers of Yeshua named Matthew was in Rome at that time having discussions with Mark. He had written a book based on Mark's with additional material and it was for the benefit of the Jews in Jerusalem. He had been a tax collector and I felt that he might be familiar with the Jewish law and court system and so I sought him out. And, since he had been a tax collector, I thought I might even sound him out on the possibility of tax fraud on the part of the priestly class. After all, they could justify such conduct on the basis that the money was being kept for their God – what they call "*Corban*"!

Dónal Questor

Dónal's diary.
Well, if Yeshua was right…and I don't for a moment believe what he is alleged to have said. But, if in the belief world of the Jews he was right then they were in big trouble for not accepting him. On the other hand, if, again in their belief world, he was wrong then he needed to be eliminated. The fact was that he had painted them as hypocrites and had accused them of "being in error because they did not know the Scriptures or the power of God". In the light of this statement in public and his confounding of their experts (again in public) it is easy to see why they were furious enough to want him annihilated. I still suspect that the tax thing may also have been on their minds! Apparently if you Corban something (that is, promise it to God), then you can't use it for anything else – not even to pay taxes!

IX.
"The enemy within?.
Rome.
[Another King of Israel?]

I met with Matthew and, for starters, I asked him what the opening of his book was about. It seems quite boring and consists of a list of over forty names from Abraham to Yeshua. It seems of no consequence. He explained that it was to show that Joseph was descended from Abraham, the founding father of the Jews and from David, the King of the Jews. At the time of the Babylonian conquest the next King of the Jews, Jechoniah, had to go into hiding. His successors to the Davidic throne have remained in hiding. Joseph, the humble carpenter from Nazareth was of The House of David and was the legitimate king of the Jews!

This was why King Herod was so scared when he heard that a king had been born to the Jews and why he ordered the slaughter of the innocents. It was because of this impending slaughter that Joseph fled with his family to Egypt. Joseph returned when he learned that Herod was dead.

He decided not to return to Bethlehem because Herod's son, who was as bad as his father, was king there. He picked Nazareth as an insignificant out-of-the-way place where he and his family could live in peace.

When Joseph died his adopted son, Yeshua, became King of the Jews. But it was not this earthly kingship in which Yeshua was interested. He wished to bring the Kingdom of Heaven to Earth so that His Father's will would be done on Earth as it is in Heaven and to rescue humans from the dominion of Satan.

It was for this reason that he demonstrated the depth of his love for humans by the terrible scourging and crucifixion that he endured. He died for humankind and rose from death glorified. He showed his followers that there is life after death and ascended into Heaven.

Dónal Questor

Dónal's diary.

This is startling news. Yeshua was not just a nondescript nobody making a nuisance of himself with the establishment. He was the rightful king of the Jews. And he had often said things like "the Kingdom is near". He was very disrespectful to the members of the establishment who were collaborating with Rome. He kept showing them up. He threatened to destroy the Temple. Would they have known or suspected that he was the legitimate King in the line of David? What would happen to them if the masses proclaimed him? Remember that small demonstration when he entered the city just before Passover. Whatever about the High Priests it seems that Pilate was not aware of Yeshua's kingship. If he had been, then he surely would not have hesitated in having him crucified. There are two supreme ironies here. The crime of which he was falsely accused by the Chief Priests was that he said that he was the King of the Jews. And the notice that Pilate put on the cross read, "This is Yeshua, the King of the Jews". Now that Yeshua has died leaving no heir to his throne who would be next in line to be king? What if the Christian Jews and the gentile Jews know who this person is and are plotting to replace Rome with this person? And might there be similar valid pretenders to the thrones in other occupied territories? Already these Christians refuse to pay homage to Caesar. I need to do further investigation.

X.
Matthew's version of Yeshua's trial.
Rome.
[Was there a miscarriage of justice?]

From another discussion with Matthew this is how I understand the Jews operate their civil law system. Although they do not seem to make any distinguishments between religious beliefs and civil law.

The Great Sanhedrin is the supreme judging authority – equivalent to that of our beloved emperor. The members come from the chief priests, scribes and elders plus the high priest who is in charge and there are 72 members. The members are Sadducees and Pharisees and the Sadducees predominated at the time of Yeshua's trial. They sit in a semicircle (so that they can see one another) in an amphitheatre. Two judge's clerks stand before them and three rows of sages sit before them. It must be an intimidating array of judges to have to face.

Although the Sanhedrin is the final authority on Jewish law it no longer has the power to execute convicted persons. That power is reserved for the Roman governor and that is why Yeshua was crucified rather being stoned to death which would have been the penalty under Jewish law.

Caiaphas was the high priest and president of the Sanhedrin at the time of Yeshua's trial and execution. As a Sadducee, Caiaphas did not believe in bodily resurrection. He would have been shocked to hear the claim that Yeshua had raised Lazarus from the dead. It was that report which seems to have been what brought issues with Yeshua to a head.

According to Matthew Caiaphas had advised the Jews that it was better to have one person die for the people rather than that the people be led astray. Therefore, said Matthew, he would not have been interested in the truth preferring to destroy what he saw as a distorter of their beliefs (*and a serious threat to his position in the community, I thought*). Jewish law is extremely strict regarding evidence acceptable in court. In cases entailing physical punishment, no circumstantial evidence, confession, or self-incrimination is recognized.

Jewish law knows of no lawyers. After the facts are presented, the court investigates, deliberates, and makes its decision by voting. Both sides have to be treated equally. Each side can be heard only in the presence of the other. In the trial procedure of capital cases, there should be a clear tendency toward bias in favour of the defendant. Thus, only the judges can argue for conviction, but all present can argue for acquittal. The most junior judges vote first so that they will not be unduly influenced by their seniors. A majority of one is sufficient for acquittal, but a majority of two is necessary for conviction. A verdict of acquittal can be reached on the same day but one of conviction only on the following day.

The rigorous cross-examination of witnesses and the warning of impending punishment that the transgressor has to receive makes it almost impossible to reach a death verdict.

"*So, Yeshua got a fair trial*" I said to Matthew.
"*Absolutely not*" retorted Matthew, "*Anything but. There was a rush to judgement. I'll tell you what happened.*"
He paused for breath and I could see that he was quite agitated.
"*Yeshua was betrayed by one of his apostles and arrested after darkness had fallen. There was a bit of a skirmish between the Jewish police who had come to arrest him and his followers but Yeshua intervened, made peace and went voluntarily with the police.*

For some unknown reason they took him to the house of Ananias, the father-in-law of Caiaphas and who had been deposed from the position of High Priest some 15 years before. Ananias' examination failed to produce any evidence of secret activity on the part of Yeshua against the Jewish or Roman authorities. In any case, Yeshua manifested neither the guilty bearing of a criminal nor the servility typical of defendants.

He was then taken before the Sanhedrin and Caiaphas, although not at the usual meeting place, but in Caiaphas' house. The legality of these proceedings seems to me to be very doubtful - the court was assembled at very short notice - it is probable that there was not a full attendance by all of the members of the Sanhedrin - no witnesses in favour of Yeshua were called. In the event however, the testimony of the witnesses for the prosecution was legally invalid because their depositions were fragmentary and confused and failed to agree in several details. Yeshua's refusal to defend himself against these accusers is an indication that he was aware of the futility of offering any defence against those whose purpose was obvious.

Having failed to adduce damning evidence from competent witnesses, the Sanhedrists realized that other means were necessary in order to achieve the desired conviction. The high priest himself then demanded personally that Yeshua state unequivocally whether he was the Messiah, the Son of God, i.e., the divinely appointed leader of national restoration and inaugurator of the messianic era described in the writings of the Prophets and more prominent in the expectations of later Judaism from the Machabean period onward. Just as directly, Yeshua answered in the affirmative and compared himself to the imagery in Daniel and Psalms, both of which passages vindicate the regal power of dominion to the legitimate representative ("son") of God.

Yeshua's reply was his death warrant. His judges declared Him guilty of blasphemy and liable to the extreme penalty of death. The Sanhedrists who condemned Yeshua did so by reference to the broad and intolerant notion of blasphemy characteristic of the Sadducean legalists whose influence predominated within the Sanhedrin at the time of Yeshua's trial.

This plot against Yeshua was the culmination of a long period in which the dominant establishment had observed Yeshua's growing popularity and their proportionately diminishing influence.
Under Roman rule, however, this sentence of the Sanhedrin was only declaratory; the execution of it was reserved to the procurator, who, as representative of the Roman Imperial Court, reserved to himself the "jus gladii". It was therefore necessary to obtain from Pontius Pilate the confirmation of the sentence and its execution.

Once again, we see the duplicity of his accusers. They had condemned Yeshua to the death penalty on the religious grounds of blasphemy. Obviously, they could hope for no execution unless Yeshua was convicted of a capital violation of Roman law of a political nature. The judges thus charged Yeshua before Pilate with stirring up the people, forbidding payment of taxes to Caesar, and declaring himself a king. Pilate's judgment was that Yeshua was not guilty of any crime against Roman law. Upon the insistence of the accusers, he continued to consider the case, interviewing Yeshua privately, sending him to Herod Antipas, offering to release him in virtue of the traditional Passover amnesty, and allowing Yeshua to be scourged in the hope that this limited punishment would placate the accusers and allow himself to be absolved of further involvement in the case.

Although in the course of private interviews with Pilate, Yeshua had acknowledged his claim to the title of king, Pilate apparently saw in Yeshua's insistence either a religious claim which he considered an internal affair of the Jews, or a delusion, but hardly a likely source of insurrection.
Finally, however, Pilate submitted to a threat from the Jews that his releasing of Yeshua would be reported to the Imperial Court in Rome as a failure to crush a possible sedition since Yeshua's acknowledged claim was to the title of Messiah, King of the Jews. This threat, coupled with the insistence of the crowds, whom the Sanhedrists had incited to demand Yeshua's death, finally led Pilate to dismiss the matter as quickly and easily as possible, i.e., by acquiescence. He therefore issued the condemnatory order, confirming the death sentence, and assigning crucifixion, the usual Roman form of execution for treason".

We paused for some moments while I gave Matthew time to regain his composure.
"*Look*" I said, "*I'm a reporter and so I need some evidence. So far, I only have your word for what happened. Not that I am doubting you, but I need another source of information.*"
"*The only person I can think of is Joseph Contraversious. He was a Pharisee and was a member of the Sanhedrin,*" said Matthew.
"*Sounds good, where would I find him?*"
"*He brought the Good News to Glastonbury.*"
"*Where is that?*"
"*Brittainia*".
Well, I thought, that is a bit too far away to travel to on the off chance of getting confirmation of Matthew's story. And, of course I was "*persona non grata*" there. Besides, he mightn't even be there at the time of my visit. Seeing the disappointment in my face Matthew continued with,
"*I believe he may be resting in Assisium at the moment.*"

"Oh! Well, that's worth a try. Can you tell me anything about him?"

"Not much. He is also known as Joseph of Arimithea. It was he who provided Jesus with a tomb and, along with Nicodemus, helped to entomb him."

"That's enough for me. If he is in Assisium I'll find him. Thank you for your information and help."

I'm not sure that there is much of interest to our readers in this matter. The Jewish authorities had a travesty of a trial because this man was drawing their followers away from their control and was claiming to be God. I suppose he was bad, mad or God.[3] He certainly wasn't bad judging from what I had heard about him. And, if he was mad, why kill him? The potentially enormous problem was that if one excludes badness and madness then he is God. For my part I reckon that he might have appeared a bit mad because his teachings were quite provocative. Pilate didn't think that he was bad and that if he was claiming to be the God of the Jews what did that matter to Rome. What a pushover that phony governor, Pilate, was. He knows that Yeshua is innocent and so he tries to mollify the Jews by having him scourged to within a centimetre of his life. That doesn't work with the rabid accusers and so he has him crucified out of fear of what they might report to his superiors. Obviously there has been a miscarriage of justice, but does it matter in the long term? A nobody in a distant land murdered through malice and incompetence.

I suspect that it may not be of any great import for you, dear readers. But to bring this investigation to a conclusion I'm off to Assisium in the morning.

Dónal Questor

---

[3] C.S. Lewis. *"Jesus was Mad, Bad, or God"*.

Dónal's diary.

I think this story is going to fizzle out and will have been a complete waste of my time. I mean, this head man, Peter, who supposedly said Yeshua was the Son of God deserts him when the going gets tough. Apparently the rest of them also went to ground. And one of the first fellows he picked and put in charge of the common purse sold him out. If he was God, how could he not have known that this would happen? And, if his father was an almighty God why didn't he rescue him from torture and death? And if he rose from the dead and was immortal why didn't he exact some revenge on his killers – or, at least confront them?

You can tell that he wasn't a Roman!

And, so much for his faithful loving followers!

I'll meet with this Joseph fellow anyway and see what he has to say.

X1.

The testimony of Joseph of Arimathea.
Assisium.
[I meet with Joseph, a man of integrity.]

Assisium is a small town perched on the lower slopes of Mount Subasio. It looks out over a plain dotted with Olive trees interspersed with occasional Oak trees. The air here is said to be therapeutical due to the sacredness and health of the land. Many of the Roman aristocrats have villas here in which they like to spend their rest periods.
As one gazes out over the plain at twilight one is conscious of a pervading stillness and tranquility.
But, enough. I was there on business.
It turned out that Joseph was staying as a guest in the villa of Tertius, a prominent Roman Senator.
Access to the villa was a little difficult since the senator was being guarded by a unit of the Senatorial Defence Corps. Eventually, I was able to persuade their leader to usher me in to meet with Joseph who was resting beside the pool.
He looked as if he needed to rest. He was quite old and had a pale wrinkled face. His emaciated arm trembled as he wearily motioned for me to sit beside him.
I introduced myself and explained that I was seeking confirmation of an account of the trial of a Nazorean by the name of Yeshua that I had been given by one of Yeshua's earliest followers named Matthew. Well, at the sound of the name "*Yeshua*", he livened up and, directing suspicious eyes into mine asked,
"*Why do you want to know?*"
I explained that I was doing a series of articles on the Christian Jews. From what Matthew had told me it seems there may been a miscarriage of justice in Yeshua's case. I needed to corroborate that account and believed that he could

help if, as Matthew had said, he had been a member of the Sanhedrin that convicted Yeshua.

"*What did Matthew tell you?*" he asked.

I recounted the tale and I think he was impressed that I did so in consultation with the notes I had made.

"*Yes. He was crucified*" – there were tears in his eyes as he said this.

"*I know that - I have been able to verify that from independent sources. What I want to know is...*"

"*But he rose from the dead three days later. He lives...*" interrupted Joseph, rising to his feet, holding his hands aloft and gazing skywards.

"*Well, that's another story. What I...*"

And now his arms were outstretched towards me and his gaze was upon me.

"*No! That is THE story. It is not **a** 'story'. It is a fact. It is what gives meaning to everything. Yeshua lives. He sits at the right hand of God. One day soon we shall see him coming in glory as a Son of Man*".

He stopped, his eyes gazing skywards. I kept silent – let him regain his composure. Minutes passed.

Eventually he said,

"*Later, the High Priest and all the council were trying to stop the apostles from spreading the word about Yeshua and his resurrection and they summoned them before the council. There was on the council a Pharisee named Gamaliel, a teacher of the law held in honour by all the people. He had been teacher to our beloved Paul as Paul trained to be a Pharisee. He gave orders to put the apostles outside for a little while. Then he said to the council, 'Men of Israel, take care what you are about to do with these men. For before these days Theudas rose up, claiming to be somebody, and a number of men, about four hundred, joined him. He was killed, and all who followed him were dispersed and came to nothing. After him*

Judas the Galilean rose up and drew away some of the people after him. He too perished, and all who followed him were scattered.
So, in the present case I tell you, keep away from these men and let them alone, for if this plan or this undertaking is of man, it will fail; but if it is of God, you will not be able to overthrow them. You might even be found opposing God!'
They took his advice for a while".
"So?" I asked.
"That was over 20 years ago. See how many now follow Yeshua's teaching – rich and poor, Jew and gentile, male and female, people from every nation in the world."

"But, can't they see that he was a failure?" I countered. "Do you think that a king or emperor would stand idly by while a bunch of misbegotten scoundrels tortured and killed his son? And, if he hadn't prevented it for some reason wouldn't he set out and annihilate the miscreants as soon as he became aware? Open your eyes, man. He was just a good talker for the ignorant. He told them things that they would like to hear and they enjoyed the way in which he thumbed his nose at the establishment. He was an entertainer. Yes, he seemed to possess a certain charisma, but that was it. He couldn't have been God or a god or a son of God. In fact, didn't he describe himself as 'a son of man'? Of man!"
There was silence for a while and I began to think that I had put him straight. But, no, he eventually began to talk.
"I do not wish to insult you. Please simply listen to what I say – you do not have to agree, just hear me out".
He paused. I nodded.
"As you know we believe that there is only one God – not many gods which is what you believe. I can understand how you can believe that there are many gods - it offers some kind of explanation for apparently random things that happen. Your gods appear to be images of certain types of persons but more

powerful. We, on the other hand believe that at the deepest level of our being each of us is an image of our one God - an image and not a part of God.

We believe that before anything existed our God was. And he created everything that exists. He created the first man and woman from whom we are all descended. Unlike other created things we have been given free will to do what is right or to do what is wrong - to live in the Truth. I think that it is quite obvious that men have done a lot that is wrong. We have become very selfish and no longer appreciate other persons as our brothers and sisters, that is, each child is a child of the one God. But, a physical child and not a Christian child. Since the dawn of creation God had not intervened. His plan was that we should have free will to construct ourselves into persons capable of enjoying the direct company of God after our sojourn here on earth, that is, after our mortal bodies die. That has not happened for the majority of mankind who rested with Hades until Yeshua freed them and the forces of evil came more and more to be in charge of the world.

Now, in what Daniel prophesied as 'the fulness of time', God has intervened. His Son, who also was God, became a human and lived with us for a short time. This was for two reasons. One was to give us an example by word and deed of how we should live in order to be a person who could be with God for eternity. And one was to present to God a perfect human being on behalf of all human beings, in effect to redeem humanity. Out of his great love for us he allowed us to give his son a heinous death in spite of which his son forgave us and showed us that we are immortal by rising from the dead and sojourning with us for 40 days.

There is a concept that, and I say this with all respect, coming from your educational background you may find difficult to understand. And that is the concept of love, of selfless love, of mercy, of non-retribution, of forgiveness. It is born out of the love that God had in creating us. That is why he created us. He first of all loved the idea of us. Then he brought us into being out of love. All he wishes for us to do is to love him and to love one another. Love operates as an attraction on the beloved - it does not control the beloved - it attracts. That is why God gave us free will, that is, so that we could be attracted to him with no control on his part. He was attracted to us by love - we certainly had no control in the matter. Yeshua gave us knowledge and an example and then became humankind's offering to God by compliance in his own death."

This, I thought, was very esoteric stuff with no foundation in fact and said,
"Well then, would you say that your one God delegates dealing with humans to the gods? I have never had any contact with this one God of yours, but I know that other gods have affected things in my life from time to time. So, it is with these gods that I must deal - they are what matters in dealing with life. When a person dies, he dies. His body rots and dissolves into the earth - rather quickly if he is cremated. You say all this speculative stuff but offer no proof."
"Yes. Firstly, it is to pause in a 'specula', that is a watchtower, and, in quietness, look and contemplate. Ask yourself 'is it possible?' Trust yourself. Identify your assumptions. Then you need Faith. And, if you want Faith, it will be given to you."
There's this "*gift*" thing again. This sounded airy-fairy to me. He's a dreamer, I thought. So, I'd wake him up.
"I like going to the chariot races", I said, "I quietly contemplate the contestants. Eventually I decide which one will likely be the winner. 'Is it possible?' I ask myself. And the answer is 'yes'. So, I trust my judgement and I speculate, I place a bet. I have faith in my choice - at least until the race is over."

"And you either win some money which is more than you wagered or you lose what you wagered?" he asked.
"Correct."
"So, what do you have to lose when you die? Something you can't take with you. But if you have faith in God, consider what you have to win."
This guy is a real smart aleck, I thought.
At that moment his host arrived and I had to leave.
"It is a difficult matter. One needs to open one's mind. But, more than that, one needs to open one's heart. Just mull it over - Dominus vobiscum" were his parting words.
My mind is in a bit of a muddle as I trudge back to my lodgings, but I will work it out.

Dónal Questor

<u>Dónal's diary.</u>
It is taking a long time to get to sleep tonight. These Christians seem to live in another world. I think they are playing mind games with me. To what end I don't know. At the same time I feel sure they don't wish me ill. They haven't sought anything from me. They don't condemn me for my beliefs. In a word, they are enigmatic.
This idea of forgiveness without retribution is arrant nonsense. Can't they see that such weakness would lead to chaos? Should we forgive the Persians for invading our lands and massacring our citizens? So, perhaps therein lies the absurdity of their beliefs.
While it explains their attitude to their followers who have been executed (and to whom they refer as "martyrs") it seems to me to be cowardice.
Maybe they will simply dwindle to extinction as happy martyrs. Problema solutum!

XI1

Can a man be a slave and be emancipated?
Assisium.
[I meet with an aristocratic slave!]

Something happened this morning. I was sitting on the terrace after a light breakfast. I was quite relaxed and at peace. Just like evening time the morning time is beautiful and tranquil in Assisium. But also, it somehow inspires hope and joy. All is new. Anything is possible. The past is done. There is only the now to be lived in while waiting for the next now. The sun rises over the plain accepting and absorbing the lifegiving water wafting up to it from the mist laden trees as they uncurl their countless leaves and turn to the sun in adoration. Energy enlivens the buds vibrating in their metamorphosis to fruit.

An elderly slave was clearing away the breakfast things. I was mildly entertained to observe the elegance with which he seemed to carry out such a menial task. He seemed happy and at ease. I smiled to myself thinking that the tranquility of Assisium knows no boundaries of race or class – its sun smiles on all.
"*What's your name, boy?*" I asked him.
"*My name is Theo, Master*" he replied. "*Theo*" I thought and I smiled inwardly wondering if I was talking with God.
"*How long have you been here?*"
"*For the past twenty years, Master.*"
"*Are you happy, Theo?*"
"*Yes, Master. Very happy, Master.*"
How could he be happy, I wondered. He has such a humdrum existence – same old, same old - day after day. Boring. No adventure. No travel. No freedom. Nothing new except

impersonal guests to wait upon. Perhaps he is mentally deficient.

"*Why are you happy, Theo?*"

"*Because God is good to me, Master.*"

I wasn't expecting an answer like that.

"*Which is your god?*" I asked, guessing that it would probably be Galinthias.

Theo straightened and with his palms and face directed to the sky said, or rather he chanted in a low resonant voice:

"The one true Lord, the God of all.
The creator of the world and all in the world
our Father in heaven
who makes his sun rise on the evil and on the good
and sends rain on the righteous and on the unrighteous.
Hallowed be His Name,
May His Kingdom come
And may His will be done on earth as it is in heaven."

Well, this certainly woke me up.

"*Are you one of these Christian Jews?*" I asked him.

"*I am a Christian, Master. A Greek gentile. A child of God. In Christ Yeshua we are all children of God. For in him we live, and move, and have our being. All of us who are baptized into Christ are clothed with Christ. There is neither Jew nor Gentile, neither slave nor free, nor is there male nor female, for we are all one in Christ Yeshua.*"

There was silence for a while. Where had I heard that phraseology before? These were the words of a fanatic. But Theo did not exhibit any of the physical signs of a fanatic – he was calm and his tone was gentle. Of course, what he was saying was arrant nonsense. Anyone could plainly see that there were Jews, gentiles, slaves, freemen, male and female. He was somewhat unhinged, I decided, and living in a fantasy world. But, might he be dangerous? Was he saying that he was an equal of me who am a free man and a Roman citizen?

"*But you're a slave.*"

"*Yes, Master.*"
"*How can you say that your god is good to you when he lets you be enslaved?*"
"*God is Wisdom. I have received the gift of Faith. I cannot comprehend why God does what he does except to know that it is permitted out of his infinite love. He will let me know what he wants me to do.*"
"*Are you saying that your god wants you to be a slave?*" I asked somewhat incredulously (at the same time thinking: there's that "*gift*" thing again).
"*Not exactly, Master. He wants me to accept it, Master.*"
"*And that's it? That is all your life is about?*"
"*Oh no, Master. I am to live as a son of my God who created me and to love him with all of my being and love my fellow men and women who are also his children, I am to trust him and in him.*"
What kind of god would want a son of his to live the life of a slave, I wondered. Of course, this poor fellow was supine, inured to the tedium of his lowly class. Totally lacking in any meaningful prospect, he had created a fantasy world for himself.
"*But you are merely a slave! You don't accomplish anything other than performing routine menial tasks that could be undertaken by anybody. I don't mean to be hurtful to you, but I can't see how you could possibly be happy. Why would this all powerful, all knowing being you postulate as the One God be interested in you? Or, interested in me for that matter?*"
He smiled.
"*Yes, Master, God is all powerful, almighty and all knowing. There is no thing that I can give to him. Anything that I might accomplish in arts, sciences or physical works can be infinitely surpassed by him. But, and I say this in humility, there is one thing that I can do for him that he cannot do.*"
Well, this caught my attention. Here was something totally at variance with the humbleness he had manifested so far. I became aware of the silence. He was waiting for me to ask him.

Well, I was curious as to what his great delusion was and so I asked him.
"*What is that?*"
"*I can of my free will love myself because God made me and I can love God for who God is.*"
Is that it I thought? Ludicrous. Is he on some kind of drugs? He thinks that there is only one god and that this god is happy to be loved by a slave. Some god that would be. Are these Christians some kind of human puppy dogs. I'd had enough and decided that I was bored. I was certainly somewhat unsettled.
"*You may leave.*"
"*Yes, Master*", and he withdrew.
I sat there musing and mulling - turning over in my mind all I'd heard from these Christians. One thing that was nagging with me was that this slave was more skilful and articulate in expressing what he thought than many educated people that I had met.

Dónal Questor

Dónal's diary.
This fellow, Theo, has the servile manner that we expect of a slave and yet, there is a dignity and composure in him that one does not encounter in slaves. I noticed the same kind of quiet confidence in members of the community I had supper with the other night. I am becoming more and more concerned as to what these Christians are up to. This fellow has that air of confidence one associates with a person who expects to prevail. Could it be that in permitting these small Christian cliques to proliferate throughout the empire that we are allowing multiple trojan horses to assemble at strategic points throughout the empire? Waiting for the day when they would be numerous and powerful enough to overthrow Rome?
Something is afoot and I am determined to get to the root of it.

XII1.

A philosopher's view.
Athens.
[I get the view of an intellectual.]

So far I have been hearing from people caught up in their religion, orthodox Jews and Christian Jews. Well, an orthodox Jew who was somewhat frenzied and another who couldn't make up his mind, and some Christian Jews with their heads in the clouds. I needed an independent view and so I have travelled to Athens, the meeting place for so many philosophers. I was looking for somebody skilled in Theodicy which I have been told is a philosophic science comprising reasoned knowledge based on principles leading to certainty and capable of justifying itself critically. In other words, what could one know about a god or gods without resorting to claims about revelations from a supernatural (unverifiable) source, or to a "*gift*"?

After some investigation it seemed that the man I should meet was a fellow called Sorcastec and I tracked him down to the shop of Simon the cobbler on the banks of the Ilissos River. I wasn't impressed when I saw him. He was of medium height and had wide-set, bulging eyes that darted sideways and enabled him, like a crab, to see not only what was straight ahead, but what was beside him as well; he had a flat, upturned nose with flaring nostrils; and large fleshy lips like an ass. Sorcastec had let his hair grow long and went about barefoot and unwashed, carrying a staff and looking arrogant. I learned that he didn't change his clothes but wore the same in the daytime as at night. There was something peculiar about his gait as well. Some said that it was a swagger so intimidating that enemies kept their distance. Apparently, he was impervious to the effects of alcohol and cold weather.

I introduced myself and told him that I was a reporter with Rumor de Mundi.

He glowered at me and grunted, "*So?*"

"*I'm investigating the difference between the Orthodox Jews and Christian Jews and would like to know your thoughts on the matter*", I said.

"*Hee-hee-hee, haw-haw-haw, ho-ho-ho, hee-hee-hee*" guffawed Sorcastec, doubling up and stomping a foot and his staff on the ground. This went on for what seemed like several minutes. Every time he stopped, he looked at me and erupted again. Eventually he looked at me,

"*Ahh, you poor wretch. You are chasing the wind. Trying to find where it started and whither it goes. The Jews made a fundamental mistake. They assumed that the one god they discovered was a person like us humans. But their god is distant from the earth and does not interfere with Rome or Greece.*"

"*Oh! So do you think that there is only one god?*" I asked.

"*Yes. I agree with Aristotle on the matter.*

The idea is this. Since forms or essences are universals, you and I may both know the same form, as we may both know the letter A. But when I actively know or contemplate that universal form, what is now before my mind is a particular: this actualization of that universal. Now consider the primary god. He is eternally and essentially the object of the active understanding that he is. So, he is a substantial particular. But since he is essentially an activity, he is also a universal essence of a special sort—one that can only be actual, never merely potential. In a way, then, the primary god overcomes the difference between particulars and universals that seemed unbridgeable. For he is at once a concrete particular and the starting-point of all scientific knowledge. He thereby unifies not just being, but the scientific knowledge of it as well, ensuring that the latter fits the former in the way that realism requires."

I just looked at him.

Please stay with me, dear reader. I asked him to repeat that several times and wrote it down as he talked. I couldn't understand what he was saying. It sounded very deep and intelligible but conveyed nothing to me except that this pagan philosopher seemed to accept as reasonable the existence of one god. But he seemed to think that this one god was not a person. I decided to probe further.

"*Oh learned and wise one,*" I toadied up to him, "*the Christians consider this one god to have become a human being some years ago and to have been executed.*"

He stared at me with his eyes agog and standing out of his head. "*Utterly irrational*" he hissed, "*fallacious, preposterous and deliriously demented.*" Pointing to the river he asked, "*Can the Ilissos be contained in an ordinary bucket? Can the universal be contained in the particular? Can the eternal be contained in the temporary? Can the infinite be executed and come to an end?*"

He was quivering with what may have been rage. I waited for him to calm down somewhat. Then, suspecting that, although I might be taunting him, I ventured:

"*But the Christians say that this god/man became alive three days after being dead and ascended into the sky.*"

"*Enough!*" he screamed walking around in small circles with his hands above his head.

I became aware that a small crowd had gathered by now and was enjoying the drama. Sorcastec seemed to be arguing with himself. He would lean forward staring ahead and mouth some silent words and then advance a metre, turn around and, again staring ahead mouth more silent words in reply. This silent pirouetting dialogue went on for quite some minutes. It was quite entertaining because his face displayed a miscellany of different expressions many of which I had never witnessed before. The crowd was enchanted. Eventually he stopped with a shout of "*As eínai. Ita sit.*"

"*We Greeks and the Romans have no problems letting nations practise their various superstitious religions provided they do not lead to civil unrest. The Jews in particular have a favourable relationship with Rome. They worship and sacrifice to a distant god in a way that does not cause any issues for Rome. And they pay their taxes. These Christian Jews, however, believe that their god is not distant. They believe that this god has come into the Roman empire in the form of a man and has threatened that his kingdom is near at hand. They believe that, although he was killed, he is still somehow alive and will deliver them from rule by Rome. Therefore, they will be seen as a threat to the stability of the empire. A boil may be only a minor irritation, but it must be burst before it intrudes into and destroys the body.*

You asked me if I considered it rational to believe there is one god. As I have explained to you, I do believe this to be rational and provable. But there is no basis for considering this god to be a person or anything like a human being with some kind of interest in this world. Quite the opposite in fact. Such worldly concerns are matters for the twelve Olympian demi-gods. If the Christians maintain that their one god is a person present to them and intent on a new kingdom then they are a threat to Rome."

With that he turned around and scuttled down the street with the crowd cheering after him.

I returned to my room at The Acropolis Inn to gather my thoughts. I summarised them as follows.

We Romans think that there are many gods. We do not have any concept of one God who is all powerful. Why should we? Instead of our disparate needs all being lumbered onto one god they are targeted at the god with particular competence in the matter to be addressed. And, we only bother with the gods when we need them to help us. And they might help or they mightn't dependant on their mood at that time. And, when you die: you die.

The Greeks seem to follow Plato's idea that God is transcendent, the highest and most perfect being, and one who uses eternal forms, or archetypes, to fashion a universe that is eternal and uncreated. Also, they think that this world isn't the real world. Some of them think we are living in a cave and dealing with shadows! No wonder they produce fellows like Sorcastec! They don't have anything to do with this one God and it doesn't have anything to do with them. Instead, they have many gods like us. But, Sorcastec did think that the Christians were a threat to Rome!

On the other hand, the Jews maintain that there is only one God who created this world and is all powerful. They believe that they were chosen by this God to get special treatment. They spend every day of their lives praying to this God and offering sacrifices to him. Some of them (called Pharisees) believe in some sort of life after death. Others (Sadducees) don't believe this and they are the ones in control (subject to Rome) in the country. Beats me how they can believe they are chosen by their God when they have been a subjugated people for centuries.

The Christians are basically Jews who believe that their God became a man and has delivered or rescued them. They all believe in life after death. What did this God/man rescue them from? I don't know. They are still under Roman rule and in acrimonious conflict with orthodox Jews. And, Sorcastic did suggest that the Christians are a threat to Rome.

Dónal Questor

Dónal's diary.

I can't get rid of this feeling that I'm missing something with these Christian Jews. Everything about them is paradoxical. It may be that the answer lies in finding out more about what that fellow Yeshua said or did. They seem to draw their inspiration from him. If he was a nobody why are the orthodox Jews so concerned about him and what he said? Maybe I can unravel the matter with some help from Mark who seems to have been collecting anecdotes about him.

I can't escape the persistent probe asking: "is it possible?". And, of course it isn't. But…

I can't get to sleep. What if? Does it really matter? Are these probes offers of that "gift" the Christians talk about? Maybe I just need to go to Pompeii for a good holiday and forget the whole thing. Some wine, women and song may be the answer.

What does it matter anyway?

X1V.

More philosophy.
Athens
[I meet a "practical" philosopher.]

After breakfasting I was sipping some posca as I relaxed on the veranda of the Quo Vadis Inn when a very old man who was unusually short in stature approached and enquired if he could join me for a chat. He had heard about my enquiries regarding Christians and felt that he might enlighten me somewhat. Why not, I thought, and beckoned the waiter to bring him a glass. He demurred saying he did not partake and thanked me profusely for the offer.

His name was Aaron Becus. He was of the Stoic school and practiced as a Coherency Balancing Thinker ("*CBT*" for short).
"*Basically, the Christians are Stoics. They have devolved from the Jews and have eschewed a lot of the Jewish laws and beliefs other than the belief that there is an otherworldly being they call 'God'. Well, we know that the only God is the universe, that is, humans, earth, sun, moon and stars. We are all part of god. As Democritus explained hundreds of years ago we are all made of the same atomic stuff. Postulating a God who is an almighty creator and of a different substance to physicality is a specious theory incapable of demonstration or proof. Mark you that: incapable of demonstration or proof. A figment of the imagination.*"

So there we are, I thought. There is nothing new under the sun.

"*What do you think about this Yeshua whom they say is the son of God, was killed and came to life again?*" I asked him.

He smiled. "*Several matters arise. Firstly, how could this infinite being they call 'God' be contained in a finite human body? And, if he was God, how could he be killed? There is no cogent proof that he became alive after dying - isn't it*

convenient that the allegedly risen one disappeared into the sky so soon after his alleged resurrection?"
He has a point, I thought and asked:
"*So, you think he was a charlatan?*"
"*No, no, no. I think he was a very good man, but somewhat egotistical, perhaps even with a touch of narcissism. I suspect that before he began teaching he had spent some time in Greece listening to and learning from our Stoic philosophers. Much of what he is reported to have said I would agree with. But I would tone down some of the hyperbolic rhetoric. Why should anyone 'pluck out his eye,' or 'cut off his hand' instead of modifying his way of living? I would like to have met with him to have given him some counselling*" he smiled.
"*What about all the miracles he is said to have performed?*" I asked him.
"*He seems to have had a powerful charisma. So, he would be convincing - especially for uneducated peasants. He probably started off his healings with something simple like getting an apparently lame person to walk where the person's paralysis had in fact been brought about by a negative mental outlook. And, of course we don't hear anything about how long the alleged cures lasted or about attempts that failed.*"
"*What about raising people from the dead?*" I asked.
"*That's easy. They weren't dead.*"
I wasn't there to defend Christians or Yeshua but I found myself getting somewhat annoyed with Aaron. He was a bit too smug and complacent for my liking.
"*So, you are saying that it is impossible that there is one God, a God who is not of this world, who is not physical, are you?*"
He blinked. I could see that his mind was racing. Probably suspected a trap. He obviously didn't like being backed into a corner.
"*No, I'm not saying that.*"
"*Therefore, you would say that it is possible, would you?*"
More silence while he considered his options.

"No."

"Let me try and understand your position, Aaron. You don't think that it is possible that there is one God and at the same time you don't think that it is impossible. Is that it?"

Silence.

I have to confess that I was enjoying myself.

"In other words, it is not possible and not impossible. If we omit the negatives isn't that saying that it is possible and impossible at the same time?"

He was literally squirming in his chair as he wrestled with his thoughts. Suddenly his face brightened and leaning towards me with his benign smile restored he sermonized in lofty tones:

"It is possible in abstract conceptual terms - much as the idea of a flying turtle is. But it is impossible that such a thing could exist in reality."

That caught me for a moment or two. But I recovered.

"I think that you are playing with words, Aaron. A turtle by definition cannot fly. If, however there were an animal to all intents and purposes like a turtle but also having wings and the ability to fly some might call it a 'flying turtle' but others would recognise it as distinct and call it something like a 'flurtle'. After all we don't call an Unicorn a horned horse with wings."

He blinked. But he didn't relent.

"Well, I think that's what the supposed concept of God is. It is like trying to talk about a square circle. And not even that since the concept is not properly defined."

"One cannot define the infinite", I retorted.

"Well, there you are then. If we can't define what we are going to discuss then we can't discuss it."

He wasn't going to get off that lightly, I thought. And I let him have it.

"That is an arbitrary statement posing as an axiom! We can start off with a general preliminary form of definition and through dialogue seek to modify and refine it. I'll give you a start: the God that the Christians and Jews talk about is a

living non-physical being that existed before the universe began and has power over everything and everyone."
"Is he good?"
"Yes."
"Does he need anything?"
"No."
He stood up, thrust his face towards me and with staring eyes and a sullen demeanour (not the least bit stoical) said,
"So why would he have created anything? And, even if he had, why a world like this one where there is so much evil and misery?"
Turning on his heel he departed before I could formulate a reply.
I sat there for quite a while mulling over what he had said.
I certainly have some cogent questions for these Christians. Maybe they are indeed Trojan horses – multiple Trojan horses. If so, dear readers, rest assured I will expose them.

Dónal Questor

Dónal's diary.
Again, I'm finding it difficult to get to sleep. What if the Christians are reading my articles? Is my life in danger? Intellectually I believe that it isn't since that would draw the attention of the authorities to them – particularly in view of my articles. Nevertheless, someone like me travelling through the empire could easily meet an end that would be construed as an unfortunate accident! I'll head back to Rome tomorrow and discuss with my editor. I have to say that I much prefer their approach to that of the bumptious Aaron.

XV.

Indian Christians?
Benevento.
[I meet an apostle.]

We left Patra at dawn anticipating that it would take two to three days to get to Brindisi on the coast south of Rome. As it happened the weather was foul and the voyage lasted four days. I must admit that due to the violence of the tempest in which we became engulfed I followed prayers to Neptune with pleas to the Christian's god...just in case! Wasn't there some story about him quelling a storm and walking on water? Neither prayer worked for me! Yes, you may well smile, dear readers. Eventually the storm simply moved off to annoy and terrify some other seafarers. Fearless once again, we sailed on.

As soon as we docked, I headed for the comfort and luxury of Antico Albergo, checked in and headed straight for their thermae[4] and some soothing water and olive oil. And, of course to sample the local gossip! This was followed by a sumptuous meal of roast pork, vegetables and cheese, washed down with that favourite wine of Caesar Augustus, Setinum. And, at last a good night's sleep. Next morning I felt human again and decided to rest there for the day before the two-week trek to Rome.

The following day we set off on the Via Appia and, after a week, we reached Benevento at midday. There I had lodgings as a guest of an old friend, a retired centurion by the name of Cornelius.

He was a Christian and, some years ago, had claimed to me that his young servant, Juvenal, had been cured by Yeshua. Of course I investigated. I discovered that Yeshua had never gone

---

[4] A complex of rooms designed for public bathing, relaxation, and social activity that was developed to a high degree of sophistication.

to the servant, that Cornelius was with Yeshua when Juvenal recovered and that Yeshua had simply said that he was cured.[5] Quite obviously there was no miracle involved, but, if it made them happy to believe that there had been what harm was there in that?

Cornelius had adopted Juvenal as his son and Juvenal had organised an ekklesia in Benevento with the help of Epaphroditus, a colleague of Paul of Tarsus. (As I have remarked: these Christians appear to be everywhere throughout the empire).

There was another guest in the house at that time - a man by the name of Bartholomew who had been an apostle with Yeshua. I learned that he was spending a few days apprising Juvenal in regard to happenings with Christian communities throughout the empire. He was on his way to India. To a city named Kashi on the river, Ganges.

At dinner that night I asked Bartholomew why he was going to India.

"*Our Lord's words to us as he departed this world in human form were that we should 'go therefore and make disciples of all nations, baptizing them in the name of the Father and of the Son and of the Holy Spirit, and teaching them to obey everything he has commanded us', to love God and forgive our neighbour.*", he replied.

"*Bu, India is so far away*", I responded.

"*That is so. But they are a very religious people. From what we have heard their beliefs are similar to ours, but lacking the full truth given to the Jews by God and revealed and brought to fruition in Yeshua. I believe I can bring great joy to them by opening their eyes to the full Truth.*

They are far more numerous than us Jews and they believe in one God whom they call Brahma who created the universe and in whom there are two other equal Gods; Vishnu who preserves the universe and Shiva who transforms the universe. Doesn't

---

[5] Luke 7:1-10

that sound a bit like Father, Son and Holy Spirit? They are near to the truth and I believe that they will welcome with great joy the revelations of the Son of God who has visited us to show us 'the Way, the Truth and the Life'. While I believe that it is possible to be saved by implicit desire (voto vel desiderio) in the case of persons of good will who would join the church if they only knew it was the one, true church of Christ, I wish to bring them the Good News and invite them to join us. To enjoy a more full life in communion with Yeshua."

All of this was over my head. What I was thinking was that not only were these seventy-five million Indians far more numerous than the Jews, they were far more numerous than us Romans. They could pose a formidable threat to the empire if they decided to supplant our gods and our way of life.

"And you, Dónal, what do you believe in?" asked Juvenal, interrupting my uneasy reverie. I stared at him. Hmm, I asked myself: what exactly do I believe in. I became aware of eyes gazing at me expectantly and found myself becoming quite irritated. So, I erupted with:

"Well, I can tell you what I don't believe", I retorted. *"I don't believe that there is one supreme all-powerful God. The world wasn't created - it was always in existence. It is nonsense and self-contradictory to say that something could be made out of nothing. And, I hope this doesn't offend you, even if there were such a God he couldn't become a human being - again a contradiction in terms. And, if there were such a wonderful all-powerful God as you speculate why would there be so much evil and injustice all around us all of the time. And, there is no reason at all to believe that a person comes alive again after he dies - lives in some kind of nirvana - lives forever - doing what? What you preach is like subduing people with opium rather than force of arms. It robs them of their dignity as men. I intend to live as a free man and a Roman and hope that the gods will treat me favourably - if they don't, well then, they don't and*

that's my bad luck. As we say in Rome: 'eat, drink and be merry for tomorrow we die". In short, I believe what my senses tell me. I don't believe in 'supposing this and supposing that'."

And then I'm afraid I made a mistake, dear readers, for I went on:

"I'd like to know what you Christians are really up to. This lovey-dovey stuff and professing to like poverty and love your enemies doesn't make any sense to me. But there must be a reason for establishing cliques throughout the empire. I believe there is an ulterior motive in your ganging up together. And I ..."

I stopped there, concerned that I might have said too much. After all, if they were conspirators in a treasonous scheme then they might see me as a threat to be disposed of.

"Sorry..." I muttered.

There were no signs of any animosity. On the contrary they looked saddened. There was silence. After a few minutes Bartholomew said:

"That is all right. You are right to believe what you think to be true. God will love you for being true to yourself. We will pray for you. I adjure you to continue to seek truth because the truth will set you free. Now it is late and we have an early start tomorrow so I bid you a good night's rest."

With that we retired to our rooms – them to rest with their God – me to rest with Somnus.

Dónal Questor

<u>Dónal's diary.</u>

I am apprehensive about going to sleep tonight. Last night I had a very disturbing dream – a nightmare. Sorcastec's face filled my vision sneering pitilessly at me and taunting me over and over with "What is truth? What do you believe?" Eventually his face dissolved into gloomy grey clouds. But I couldn't get his words out of my mind. What does he mean: "what is truth?" Well, as our motto says: "Shining a spotlight on what citizens need to know".. And that is what I am doing in regard to these Christians. I'm shining a light and getting the facts. Or, am I? So far all I seem to have gotten is unverified hearsay evidence – except in the case of Peter and to a lesser extent Paul, Matthew, Joseph and Mark. But, aren't they biased? Of course one may equally ask: "where is the evidence for Apollo and the other gods?" It was quite a while before I eventually fell asleep that first day.

Another restless night after the second day. More confused dreams. Thankfully the anathematic Sorcastec did not put in an appearance. But over and over I was harassed by "What is truth?" and "what do you really believe?". "To what are you committed?" Over and over until mercifully sleep liberated me. I fear that it is only a temporary truce.

And what is this stuff about the truth setting me free. My job is seeking the truth and letting our readers know about it. Don't worry I'll be doing that whether or not you like it, Bartholomew. And "free"? Why, I am free – a free man of Rome – more free than you Christians.

XV1.

Historical source and a phony.
Benevento.
[A non-Christian source.]

On Tuesday morning Cornelius introduced me to a very interesting document. It was an excerpt from a history written by a highly respected historian named Josephus and ran in part as follows:

About this time comes Yeshua, a wise man. For he was a worker of incredible deeds, a teacher of those who accept the truth with pleasure, and he attracted many Jews as well as many Greeks. And when, in view of his denunciation by the leading men among us, Pilate had him sentenced to a cross, those who had loved him at the beginning did not cease. And even now the tribe of the "Christians" – named after him – has not yet disappeared.

So, Josephus reported that Yeshua was wise, good and virtuous and that many became and remain his disciples. Well, I think that I have discovered that much myself.

Several things to note:
- "*Messiah*" (a Hebrew word) and "*Christ*" (a Greek word) both mean "*the anointed one*". The reason one is anointed is because he is going to be king.
- Does "*incredible deeds*" mean? "*miracles*"?;
- No indication that Yeshua was or claimed to be the Son of God as the Christians claim;
- No reason given as to why Pilate condemned him.
- No mention of any involvement by the Sanhedrin. But then Josephus was a Pharisee and if Matthew's account was correct, one could understand why he might not report on their involvement. Makes one wonder what else he may have failed to report.

> Publisher's note.
> A brief note on Josephus.
> Born 37 C.E. died 100 C.E.
> Josephus was a Jew and a pharisee. In 64 C.E. Josephus was sent to Rome to secure the release of a number of Jewish priests who were held prisoners in the capital. There, he was introduced to Emperor Nero's second wife, whose generous favour enabled him to complete his mission successfully. Josephus was deeply impressed with Rome's culture and sophistication—and especially its military might.
> In 67 C.E. he was engaged in a revolt against the Romans and managed to hold the fortress of Jotapata for 47 days, but after the fall of the city he took refuge with 40 diehards in a nearby cave. They voted to perish rather than surrender. Josephus, arguing the immorality of suicide, proposed that each man, in turn, should dispatch his neighbour, the order to be determined by casting lots. Josephus contrived to draw the last lot, and, as one of the two surviving men in the cave, he prevailed upon his intended victim to surrender to the Romans.
> Taken as a prisoner to Rome he managed to wheedle his way into the emperor's favour and from that time on attached himself to the Roman cause.
> Josephus' first wife had been lost at the siege of Jotapata, and his second had deserted him in Judaea.
> While in Alexandria with the emperor he married for the third time.
> Later he divorced his third wife and married an aristocratic heiress from Crete,
> Personally, Josephus was vain, callous, and self-seeking. There was not a shred of heroism in his character, and for his toadyism he well deserved the scorn heaped upon him.

I thanked Cornelius for his help and apologised for my somewhat intemperate outburst at dinner the previous day. I met with Juvenal and Bartholomew also and expressed my regret to them. All were magnanimous in response and, having thanked Cornelius and Juvenal for their hospitality I set off towards Rome.

Monte Cassino.
[I meet with some charlatans.]

We stopped to rest for a day at a pleasant country inn in Monte Cassino. Word must have gotten around that a newspaper reporter was in town because, after refreshing myself and while I was reclining on the veranda, I was approached by a local.

"*Sir*", he said somewhat deferentially, "*please forgive this intrusion. My name is Titus and I ask you to join us for dinner this evening. We are a small group of Christians and would be most grateful if you would write about us in your newspaper*".

Well, I was tired and, I confess, a bit grumpy. I had been looking forward to a nice meal and an early retirement to bed. "*Look,*" I said, "*I'm tired. And I've already dined with some Christian groups and written about their beliefs.*"

"*Well, that's it*". replied Titus, "*we disagree with some of the things that you have written about Yeshua and God. We want to set the record straight. That is, we want your newspaper to set the record straight, to correctly shine your spotlight on what citizens need to know*".

I can tell you that he now had my undivided attention.

"*In what respect?*" I asked.

"*We will explain over dinner. Please come.*"

"*All right.*"

"*I'll call for you at sunset.*"

Titus arrived just before sunset. Thankfully he came in a chariot as our destination lay up the steep hill of Monte Cassino. The destination was impressive: a large well-appointed villa with a magnificent pool and vineyards. I was ushered in to a sumptuous dining room where, in the centre, the host and a dozen toga clad men relaxed around a veritable feast. There were four other dinner gatherings scattered around the room each also comprising a dozen men. And many servants in attendance. No women present I noticed.

I was ushered to a place at the right hand of the host. His name was Clisteor Sleeveen – and, as I discovered, it was a name that well described him. He had a great booming voice and was enamoured of exercising it and listening to it. Yes, he was impressive and all seemed to enjoy listening to him holding forth, but none was as infatuated by his oratory as himself.

"*Salve, mi amice*" he greeted me. "*We wish to correct some misapprehensions that have been reported in your articles on Yeshua. We are the true followers of Yeshua. It has been given to us to understand who he is and his message. You have been misled by the so-called followers that you have met.*"

"*Why would they wish to mislead me?*" I asked.

"*Oh, it was not intentional. It is simply that they lack full knowledge and are not enlightened. But we are. One primary error was their failure to know that all material things are evil – we consider that to be self-evident, just look at the world around you.*

They know only the God of the Jews, the God who created this material world and, as can be plainly seen, material things are evil. Their God has fooled them. But we are not to be fooled. We, the cognoscenti, know of a greater God who is pure essence and love.

When Yeshua took the disciples aside to better inform them and he also taught them secret things. But they did not understand them - he was exasperated with them asking them 'Do you still not understand?'.

However, they have passed down to us these esoteric matters and we understand them. Yeshua was not a human person - he only appeared to be. So, he was never crucified, never died and therefore didn't need to rise from the dead. After all, we are talking about the Supreme Being. It is infantile to suppose that he could be a mere human.

We, the cognoscenti, have been awakened, have studied the skies and have learned how to navigate various layers through the upper atmosphere where one's spark of spirituality can unite with the godhead."

I looked at the table and all the luscious food and wine and the finery in which they were dressed and their plumpness. Well, I thought, if material things are evil they don't seem to mind being immersed in them. This man is a charlatan, I thought. His conduct doesn't jibe with what Yeshua said about the poor, the meek, and so on. I didn't blame him for that but I knew that he wouldn't be a source of any worthwhile lowdown on what the Christian cliques might be planning to do. He was simply too full of himself. To tell the truth I was disgusted and wanted to escape the company of these pompous self-serving windbags, and, before I could help it, I blurted out:

"Oh dear. I've just remembered that a very important person is calling on me tonight. He has travelled all the way from Caesar's court and I can't keep him waiting. I must take my leave, I'm afraid. I am so sorry."

I could sense that he was about to lose his temper and quickly interjected:

"Perhaps it would be all right with you if I brought my guest to visit you in the morning to learn about your wonderful and distinguished community? I'm sure that the Emperor would wish to know more about you and your profound insights."

He calmed down immediately – probably sensing an opportunity to ingratiate himself with the powers that be.

"But, of course. Would noon be suitable?"

"Yes, excellent" I responded, and we headed for the door with him uttering *"Vale"* as I escaped and was thinking that Monte Cassino would be a long way behind me by noon tomorrow.

I scurried down the mountainside and was glad to reach the sanctuary of the inn. When I had calmed down with the collaboration of a carafe of wine I retired to my chamber.

Dónal Questor

Dónal's diary.

What a difference there is between the clique in Benevento and the one in Monte Cassino. Surely they could not be brothers in arms. And, now that I think about it, there seems to be differing understandings and interpretations of who or what Yeshua was in the various groups I had encountered. All seem to agree that he was a good person, cured many people and had wonderful teachings. But, there is deep disagreement as to whether he was a human being, or God, or some kind of combination of human and God.

Was he a human who seemed to be God?

Was he God who seemed to be a human?

How could he be both since he referred to his father (that is, God) in heaven?

I reckon that this ambiguity will result in the whole movement dying out. They are too befuddled. At this stage I have to admit that I am disappointed since we could well do with more people like some of the Christians that I have met.

Isn't that strange? Perhaps I am seeing something that I can't quite articulate or put words on? There's that little whisper again: "is it possible?" Another word that is knocking around in my head is "trust". Is trust what they mean when they say "have faith?"

Anyway, it seems like it is time to wrap up this particular assignment. (Unless of course I get a sign – ha, ha, ha).

[Editor's note: *"Be careful what you ask for".*]

<u>Silence.</u>

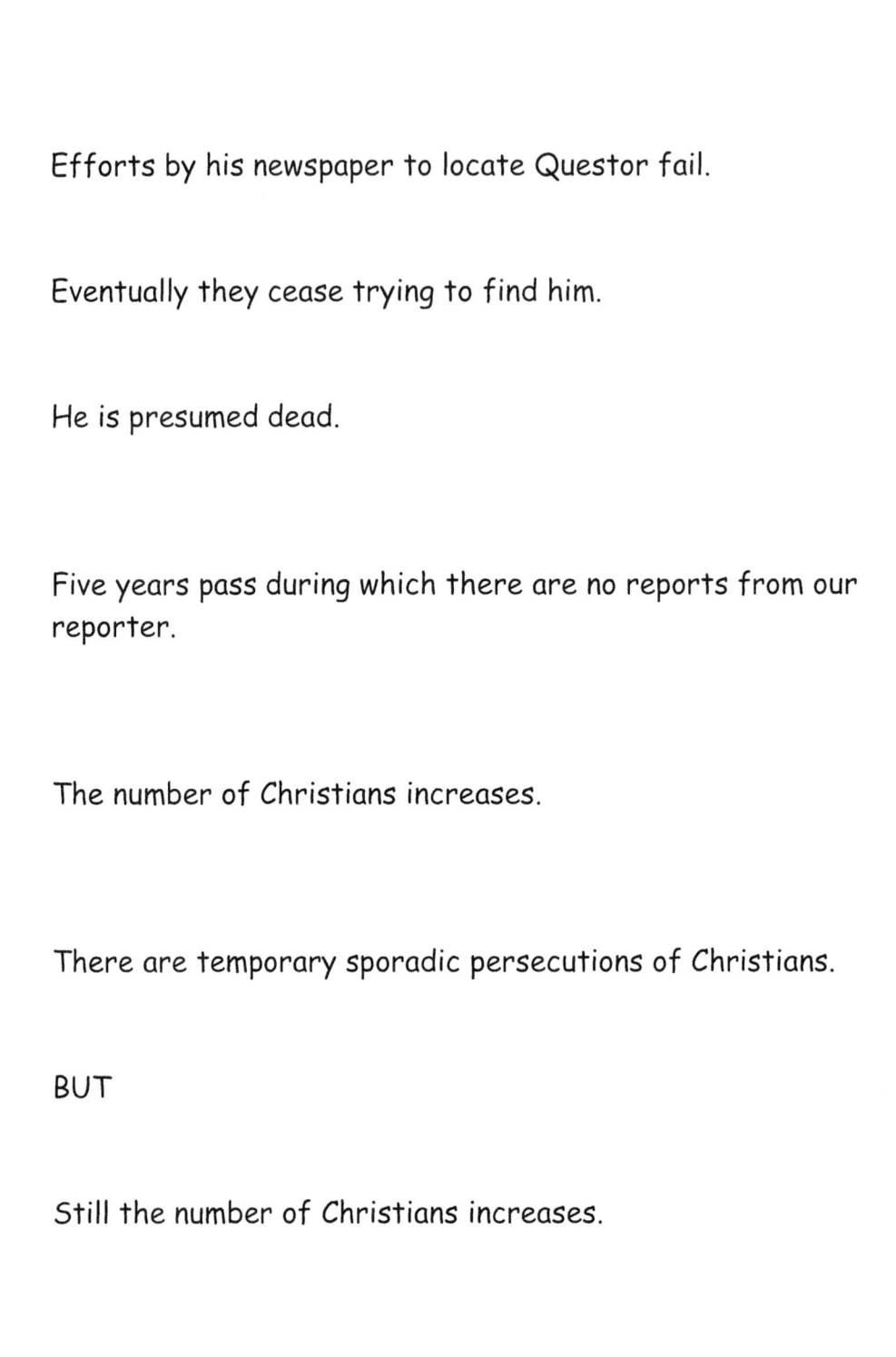

Efforts by his newspaper to locate Questor fail.

Eventually they cease trying to find him.

He is presumed dead.

Five years pass during which there are no reports from our reporter.

The number of Christians increases.

There are temporary sporadic persecutions of Christians.

BUT

Still the number of Christians increases.

> Publisher's note: there follows an account kept by our reporter and forwarded to us recently from the island of Patmós.

A life changing event.

69 CE - Five years later !!!
[*During which time all was changed utterly.*]

Patmós

Hello once again dear readers.
At last, I can write to update you.
And I am a radically different person to who and what I was when I last wrote for you.
My apologies for not reporting sooner, but it was due to circumstances beyond my control. In fact, it was impossible. But now I can tell you of my adventures – some might say, misadventures.

My journal.

Five years ago in a caravan of over a hundred fellow travellers we had set off from Monte Cassino early in the morning following my brief encounter with the Gnostics. We had just passed through Frosinone when we were set upon by a contingent of Roman legionaries. We were no match for those brutes. They hit us with clubs and knocked us to the ground. Then they shackled our hands and legs, and, I can tell you, they were very rough and noisy about it.

No explanations were forthcoming as to why we were being seized. We were frog-marched to Valmontone where we bivouacked for the night. We were given some awful gruel and left chained in a tent. It was cold. I slept fitfully being fearfully apprehensive as to what fate might await me.

At dawn we set off again and reached Rome in the late afternoon. There we were incarcerated in Mamertine Prison. What an evil place. I was totally exhausted and, notwithstanding the filth of the cells into which we had been tossed and the moans of the inmates, I fell into a deep sleep.

At dawn we were roused and given a bread roll and water. We noticed that the legionaries were no longer our gaolers. They had been replaced by a motley crew of villainous looking reprobates. What was going on, I wondered. I summoned up my courage and asked one of my fellow prisoners.

"*We've been sold to slave traders*" is what I was informed to my horror. But there has been a terrible mistake I thought. I am not a servus, a slave. I have not committed any crime. I am a free man. I know men of importance in Rome. Indeed, I myself am of no little importance and prominence. I need to put a stop to this appalling injustice.

I attempted to identify myself to one of our captors only to receive a devastating backhander which knocked me to the ground in a daze. Looking at my assailant I knew that it was better to not say another word. After being nudged several times by the brute's boot I got to my feet. He simply grunted. The first intimations of despair flickered in my heart.

Then they chained about a hundred of us together and marched us out of Rome. Although we didn't know it at the time we were heading for the port of Ostia, about thirty kilometres hence. We paused several times for a short rest and water. Many fell on the way and were callously whipped to their feet. Several couldn't get up and were abandoned at the side of the road – I do not believe that they would have survived, fodder for wolves or bears.

At last, we reached Ostia and staggered into the fort where we were allowed to collapse in the courtyard. I was at the end of my tether both physically and mentally. I managed to take in some gruel, bread and water. As I lay there nodding off a picture of Theo come into my mind. The elderly slave from Assisium was smiling and saying to me: "*He wants you to accept…*"…"*to accept*"…"*He*"…"*He wants you*"…"*He wants you"*...before I succumbed to a merciful oblivion dreaming of the inn at Monte Cassino and of wine.

It gets worse.

Dawn. I awoke. Tired and frightened. Sore. "*What now?*" I wondered. I looked around. Others were stirring. At the sides of the courtyard and on its parapets our captors stood watching over us. The guards in the courtyard were armed with swords, whips and cudgels. Those on the parapets with bows and arrows at the ready.
There were several rough wooden tables with benches scattered around the yard. We stood or sat for an hour or so shuffling around. Miserable. Wretched. I will not burden you, dear readers, with an account of the discomfiture caused by the lack of toilet facilities. After a while whispered conversions broke out among us.
"*Where are we?*"
"*What's happening?*"
"*Where are you from?*"
Then, one of the ruffians on the parapet, whom I took to be a leader, shouted out:
"*Silence. No talking. Remain where you are.*" And, to emphasise his words several of the ruffians administered lashes to those closest to them.
Silence.
"*Sit*" he ordered.
Mindful of the lashes that the unlucky few at the periphery had suffered we all sat in silence
Fear and despair were palpable.
The two huge doors in the archway opened and a dozen men pushing carts entered and emptied the contents onto the tables. Salted bread, milk, dried fruit and cheese with spoons and bowls were unloaded and placed on the tables.

It was very strange. We were ravenous and salivating at the prospect of food. But shameful funk inhibited each of us so that nobody reached for the food. I became aware of the guards remarking and guffawing and in a short time the leader bellowed at us:
"*Fools. Idiots. Cretins. Eat!*"
Which we did. Like savages. Each fearful that he wouldn't get enough. But we all ate and drank as much as we could. Sated. This is very strange, I thought. Why the sudden magnanimity? And not just bare rations – an excess of food. The young man beside me appeared to be of good breeding despite the rags and grime. I turned to him and:
"*Excuse me. Do you know what is going on? Has there been a change of heart by our captors? What next?*"
Yes, dear readers, I was babbling again. My mind was in turmoil. Remarkably one can get seemingly drunk on bread and milk if, previously, one has been starved and maltreated. But here I was most fortunate in my quest for enlightenment. He turned and, smiling, he said,
"*My name is Clement.*"
"*I'm Dónal.*"
"*Salve Dónal. Peace be with you. Be not afraid.*"
Well, this took me aback I can tell you. I was petrified with fear. And, rightly so in view of the kidnapping and brutal treatment by a pack of utter savages. I gaped at him.
"*We will be safe. The Lord will protect us.*"
"*Lord? What lord?*" I spluttered.
He smiled! Honestly. A gentle smile. I wondered if I was unlucky enough to have engaged with a mad man.
"*Yeshua, the Lord of all. We are in his hands.*"
Oh no, I thought. One of those crazy Christians.
"*Who are you?*" I demanded, "*one of those Christians?*"
"*Yes.*"

I would have left and gotten away from this lunatic except that this would have attracted the unwelcome attention of our gaolers with altogether unwelcome results.

"Let me tell you about myself. I am a Roman citizen raised in an affluent Jewish Roman family. I met the apostle Peter on the occasion of his first visit to Rome and received the gracious gift of belief in Yeshua. With Peter and others we established an ekklesia in Rome. Then I travelled with Paul on his journey to Corinth where I remained to assist with the instruction and guidance of the first Corinthian Christians. They were distinguished by humility, being in no respect puffed up with pride and more willing to give than to receive. But the worthless rose up against the honoured, those of no reputation against such as were renowned, the foolish against the wise, the young against those advanced in years. They seized me and sold me to these degenerates who have brought me here to Ostia."[6]

Just then we were interrupted and herded to one end of the courtyard where there were situated several cisterns filled with water. We were forced to undress and bathe in the waters. Afterwards we were given coarse dark woolen tunics to wear. Several horse-drawn wagons entered and we were herded aboard. Despite my misgivings about him, I managed to clamber on beside Clement.

"What is going on?" I asked him.

"We are being taken to a slave market".

Shock. Horror. What dreadful fate awaited me, I wondered. I was in a fearful panic, quaking and feeling my legs about to give way. Clement put a hand on my shoulder and whispered:

"Fear not, Dónal. You have won favour with our Lord. He will hold you in his hand and you shall not perish."

A blast of rage ousted my fear and I turned on him:

---

[6] Publisher's note: After the death of St. Peter's successors Clement took up St. Peter's position of primacy in the Church around the year 90. See First Epistle of Clement to Corinthians.

"Are you totally insane? We're going to be sold to who knows what kind of taskmaster to spend the rest of our lives, our very shortened lives, in daily grinding labour in some quarry or mill or hellhole. Tell your lord to keep his hands off me and let me die now."

Yes, readers, I had, as they say, "*lost it*". My state of mind consisted of two emotions: fear and hatred.

Clement simply put an arm around me and held me tightly until we reached a market square. There we were bundled onto a platform facing a large group of men whom I took to be slave owners or agents for slave owners. In horror I realised that we were like lots to be bid for. I'm afraid that I cannot recall much of the following events – I was in a complete daze – my mind had stopped working.

When I came somewhat to my senses I realised that I was in a cart with two others heading away from the market. I had been purchased. No longer was I a man – I was a chattel. A dreadful sense of foreboding began to well up inside me. Then I felt a hand on my shoulder and, without looking, I knew who it was.

"Easy, now. Easy brother. All will be well brother".

Clement! He really was most irritating.

Despair and hope.

In a short while we arrived at a harbour which was about three kilometres north of the mouth of the Tiber. It was an impressive sight having been constructed by Augustus about a century before. It consisted of a 150-hectare port basin with two curved piers, docks, and a multi-storey lighthouse. And, it was very, very busy – hundreds of boats loading and unloading, arriving and departing.

We were loaded aboard a merchant ship and I can remember the feeling of relief that it did not have banks of oars. My relief was short lived. We put to sea and sailed westward. My days consisted of various kinds of hard labour. What I dreaded most was having to climb up the rope ladder on the main mast to adjust the staysails. However, while the work was arduous the general conditions were tolerable. The food was wholesome and the hammocks adequate for a good night's sleep, particularly because by the end of the day one was totally exhausted.

After three days and nights we reached Massilia, a city, located on three hills overlooking a harbour which was a centre of maritime trade. It was from here that my adventures unfolded through many voyages to islands and to towns and cities in and around the Mare Nostrum. I have written of these exploits in my book, "*A Hibernian, a Roman and an Inquirer*". Over the course of the next number of weekends I wish to acquaint my readers with accounts of the several remarkable persons I was privileged to meet in the course of my travels. Please forgive me for the inadequacy of these accounts but it is beyond my powers to properly describe the harbingering nuances that affected me during those duologues.

"*I came, I saw, I conquered*" is the famous phrase uttered by Julius Caesar following his victory in the Battle of Zela in Anatolia.

My cry following several revelatory encounters in my peregrinations North, South, East and West around our sea and my victory in what I call "*The victory for the real Dónal*" was:

"*I met, I heard, I regenerated, I give thanks for the gift*".

I can never adequately thank these wellsprings of truth or Clement who patiently nurtured my ability to discern.

Rubin

Syracuse

Whenever we put into a port or travelled inland to a settlement it was the habit of Clement to induce me to accompany him to an evening meal with some of the local Christians. My first visits were made for selfish reasons – I so enjoyed the peacefulness and the congenial atmosphere – and, of course the good food! It was at one of these gatherings that I first met with Rubin. He sat himself down beside me. He was quite old, slender and of short stature. As he possessed a somewhat prominent nose and sported a rather luxuriant beard I wondered if he was Jewish.

"*Shalom*" he greeted me, "*my name is Rubin*".
Before I could say anything he shook my hand and continued, "*And yes, I am Jewish*", he said with a broad smile.
Was I that easy to read, I wondered and recovering quickly, "*Ave Rubin. My name is Dónal and I'm a Roman*".
"*Oh?*" he looked at me through arched eyebrows.
"*Well, actually I'm a Hibernian who has become a Roman citizen*".
"*And what, may I ask, is High Bernian*".
"*Hibernia is an island far to the west. It is just past Britannia and thus outside the empire. Beyond Hibernia there is nothing but sea and the unknown, possibly the edge of the world.*"
I could see that Rubin was interested in hearing about this remote island and I regaled him with stories about the various chieftains, the Fianna, Cú Chulainn and Druids. It was the Druids that caught his attention.
"*They seem to have a lot in common with us Christians*" he said. "*Although, of course, they have not had the gift of being chosen by God or visited by his Son. However, from what you have told me I think that they would be very receptive to hearing the Good News*".

Thinking about the people I knew in Hibernia I was not inclined to agree with him. But I diverted him asking,

"Are you not a Jew, Rubin?"

"Oh yes, indeed. But I am also a Christian, a believer in and a follower of Yeshua who I believe to be our long-awaited Messiah and the Son of God".

"And, do you also believe that Yeshua is God?"

"Yes".

"But, don't Jews believe that there is only one God? So how could Yeshua be God and the Son of God? Surely that is two gods?"

Rubin smiled. *"It does seem to be a paradox, doesn't it? But, while it is a paradox for us humans, that doesn't mean that it is a paradox for God. I believe that some day, probably after I die, God and Yeshua will help me to comprehend."*

I didn't understand this. It was irrational. One apple plus one apple equalled two apples, not one apple. One apple plus one orange equalled...fruit. But, not **one** fruit. So, when Jews and Christians spoke of one God, did they mean something like fruit meant for apples, oranges etc.? But we don't talk about one fruit except in relation to a single apple or banana etc. But the word fruit is only a description of what all the fruits have in common and no one fruit is the fruit. We Romans could say of our gods that there is only one order of godliness.

I realised that Rubin was gazing at me with a kindly smile and that he had a good idea of what was going through my mind.

"So, how did you, a Jew who believes that there is only one God, come to join the Christians who believe that Yeshua was also God?" I asked him.

"One word", he said, *"one word prompted my rebirth".*

I stared at him.

Waiting.

He locked onto my eyes.

"Abba", he said.

He could see from my expression that I had no idea what he was talking about. He went on:

"*'Abba' is the Aramaic word used by a child to address his or her father.*
It expresses the heart of Yeshua's relationship to God.
He spoke to God as a child to its father; confidently and securely, and yet at the same time reverently and obediently. As Yeshua said to us, 'Truly I tell you, whoever does not receive the kingdom of God as a little child will never enter it'. And I learned from His prayer that is what is required of us..."

"*To love one another*", I interrupted - somewhat scoffingly I ashamedly confess.

"*Yes*", he replied, "*but that is not what caught my attention. It was that God would forgive me my sins against God in as much as I forgave others their misdeeds against me*".

We sat in silence for a while. This man, Rubin, was quite intelligent as far as I could see – indeed like most of the other Christians that I had met. Yet...it made no sense to me that I should become childish. I wouldn't survive for very long in this hostile world if I became childish. I thought back to some of the Christians that I had encountered, Peter, Paul, Mary of Magdala, the slave Theo. They hadn't seemed childish to me. Yet, there was indeed something child-like in their approach to life, something simple yet enigmatic, implying a truth revealed to them and hidden from the rest of us. What on earth could it be? Magic? A plot to overthrow the empire? Drugs?

Rubin interrupted my wandering deliberations:

"*'Abba' is the first word in the prayer that Yeshua taught us. It changed my thinking totally and utterly. God, as I had understood him, was a mighty all-powerful king ruling his people in the same manner as one of our earthly kings. Everything about this God was about rules – and the rules were mostly negative rules. Well, of course God is a mighty and all-powerful king – but, God is my Abba and I am his child. God does not treat us as an earthly king might, but, rather as our father* would. I then reread our holy books. It was as though they were totally different books from what they had seemed to be when I had read them previously - particularly Genesis and Exodus. Our Father had rescued us from evil slavery in Egypt, nurtured us in the desert for forty years while instructing us how to live in his family and then led us once again into the land of our forefathers. Oh, if only poor Job had known that the God whom he loved despite the awful misfortunes inflicted on him, was his loving father, how different might his prayers have been."

He paused and my mind wandered. I had never thought much about our Roman gods. I did partake in the public tributes to them and asked favours every now and then. But these gods were quite impersonal and there was no way that I could envisage a filial relationship with any of them. In fact, I suppose one could regard them as whimsical having far better things to do than having anything to do with the likes of me. In truth I had not ever given them any thought unless looking to them as a last resort. I had just gone with the crowd. Now I found myself asking questions and, I have to shamefully admit, hoping those gods would not hear me doubting them. Yes, I was befuddled. And this forgiveness thing was unthinkable. I could never forgive the brutes who had abducted me, nor my jailers or those who sold me into slavery, or my present masters. Never! My mind was racing. In circles. Suddenly the world had become even more unstable and I was helplessly adrift.

"*Shalom, Dónal, shalom,*" Rubin interrupted, "*rest yourself. Repeat 'shalom' in a quiet voice and you will find peace. Say 'shalom'. Pray 'shalom', 'shalom', 'shalom*".

I did – eventually – and began to regain some composure. Then I began to get angry. What was going on? Was this fellow playing with me. Was I a fool to be giving any mind to his absurd notions?

"*Shalom, shalom, shalom*" gently from Rubin. "*God is your Abba, you are his beloved son*".

The hushed blessings had the desired effect and I became calm. We sat in silence. But! But that thoroughly aggravating question "*Is it possible...*" kept bludgeoning its way into my mind and I kept repelling it only to have it replaced by a series of "*but*"s and "*what if*"s. But the seeds had been sown:

One God,
My father,
Cares for me.
ME!

Nicodemus

Cyprus

We visited Cyprus many times. It was one of my favourite venues with its abundant sunshine, good food and wine. And, of course, Nicodemus. For it was there that I met Nicodemus, a man who was to have a great influence on my life. He was a Jew from Jerusalem where he had been a Pharisee and a prominent member of the Sanhedrin. He was now a prominent person in Cyprus and the Elder of the Christian community there.

It was the habit of Nicodemus to visit the harbour of Kition [Publishers' note: now known as Larnaka] and converse with the slaves who had landed there. It may seem strange, but, the first time I met him and was captured by his mesmerizing gaze I had an irrational feeling that he had come for the sole purpose of meeting me. Such was his presence. He introduced himself and said,

"Shalom. Next time you visit our island please come to my house and dine with me."

Somewhat shaken I replied,

"But I can't. I am a slave."

"Do not worry. I know your master and it is his pleasure to permit his slaves to visit with me."

I related the matter to Clement and he was most insistent that I go.

"Listen to him. He is a good man. He has met with Yeshua and will have much to tell you. You should regard this as your Heavenly Father's intervention in your life. Nicodemus will be God's channel to you. He will offer you a gift."

Clement meant well, but he made me nervous. What's in it for Nicodemus, I wondered. And, why would my master agree to letting me out of his supervision? But there was the prospect of a salubrious meal and somehow, I trusted Nicodemus and felt partial to meeting him again. So, I decided that I would take a chance – after all, what did I have to lose?

Nicodemus – *second meeting.*

It was two months later when I visited Nicodemus in his house. He brought me to the dinner table and introduced me to the ten guests already seated there and we sat. Then one of the guests, a lady by the name of Apphia, chanted:

Bless us O Lord as we sit together,
Bless the food we eat today,
Bless the hands that made the food,
Bless us O Lord. Amen.

And the food was good. I told Nicodemus about my background as a reporter and about how I had been waylaid and turned into a slave.

"*So, you are a seeker after truth?*" asked Nicodemus.

"*Yes. As we say: we 'shine a spotlight on what citizens need to know'*".

"*Well, I can assure you that citizens and everybody else need to know about Yeshua. That is what we Christians are about.*"

"*I see. Or, rather I don't see. What is it that allures you to a dead person who seems to have never achieved anything in his life?*"

"*Yeshua the person. Who he was. Who he still is. What he was. What he said. What he did. What he is still doing.*"

I stared at him. Here we go again, I thought. Abstruse allusions – to what? In some frustration I could feel my temper rising. Before I could say something that I might later regret Nicodemus interrupted my stream of thought:

"*It is getting late and you must depart soon. I will tell you of the first time I saw him. Then, on your next visit, I will tell you more.*"

"*Okay.*"

"*As you may know I was a Pharisee and a member of the Sanhedrin. We had heard many stories about this Nazarene. How he seemed to be some sort of magician capable of apparently wondrous deeds. How he flouted our Law and* uttered blasphemies. That he was reputed to be possessed by Beelzebub. This was all hearsay. I and my close friend, Joseph, wanted some evidence before reaching a conclusion.

I made it my business to meet with him. In secret I am ashamed to say, because I didn't want any members of the Sanhedrin to know that I was engaging with him on my own. I was very apprehensive going to him. Immediately I sensed a calmness in his company. Then that was disturbed by what he said to me. 'Very truly, I tell you, no one can see the kingdom of God without being born from above', he said. I was shocked. How could one be born again, I wondered. And again, he said, "one must be born of the Spirit". Then he looked deeply into my eyes and said, 'God so loved the world that he gave his only Son, so that everyone who believes in him may not perish but may have eternal life. Indeed, God did not send the Son into the world to condemn the world but in order that the world might be saved through him.'

We parted company soon after that and my mind was in turmoil. I called on my friend, Joseph of Arimithea, and recounted what Yeshua had said. We meditated on and discussed his words in the days and weeks after that and we witnessed his interactions with scribes in the Temple. He was so wise. In a way we wished that we could believe in him. But the stumbling block was his claim to be the Son of God."

"Well, I can understand that" I said. The mainstay of the Jews' belief is that there is only one God. So, how could a single God have an offspring? And, even if he could and did, wouldn't the son also be God? That is two Gods – not credible for a Jew.

"So, you dismissed what he had said" I said.

"Not quite" Nicodemus replied. "But we were in a kind of lacuna. We couldn't say 'yes' and we couldn't say 'no'. It was tortuous. One of the mistakes I made about him was to mistake his gentleness for passivity. Well, we were in for a shock."

"How was that?" I asked.

"*Our feast of the Passover was near and Jerusalem was teeming with visitors with many thousands camped on the surrounding hills. The Temple was full of people and a great deal of business was being carried on as the pilgrims sought lambs, doves and so on for sacrifice.*"

How well I remembered the fever of activity I had witnessed on my visit there – bedlam!

"*We were at prayer in the Priests' Court when our Minchah was interrupted by the sounds of clamour and mayhem coming from the outer court. We rushed out and, to our utter astonishment, there was Yeshua attacking the money changers and traders. Not the gentle teacher of parables at that moment. Not the curer of physical afflictions. No! He had made a whip out of cords and was driving the businessmen out of the Temple. Scattering their tables of coins, chasing the animals also and shouting: 'It is written in Isaiah, My house shall be called a house of prayer, but you make it a den of robbers'. He also spoke of the Temple as "my Father's house'. But, do you know what stuck in my mind when matters quietened down?*"

"*That maybe the rumours about him were true, that he was some kind of mad man?*" I suggested.

"*No. It was the way he said '**My** house' and '**My** Father'. It did not sound as if he was merely quoting Isaiah. It sounded like he was talking about his house! His Father's house! But the Temple is the house of God. He was claiming to be God or a son of God. We and generations before us had looked forward to the coming of a messiah, a saviour, to free us from our enemies. This had been foretold by the prophet Isaiah:*

*For a child has been born for us,
a son given to us;
authority rests upon his shoulders,
and he is named
Wonderful Counselor, Mighty God,
Everlasting Father, Prince of Peace.*

Great will be his authority,
and there shall be endless peace
for the throne of David and his kingdom.
He will establish and uphold it
with justice and with righteousness
from this time onward and forevermore.

The mention of David caused us to think of the Messiah as a great warrior who would physically vanquish our enemies. Surely this man, Yeshua, could not be such a person, could he? Most of our leaders did not think so and I was inclined to agree with them. But, the way in which Yeshua said '**My** Father' and **My** House' initiated perplexing doubts. I decided that I would meet with this Yeshua again and sound him out.
I shall tell you about that encounter next time we meet."

Jonathan.
Alexandria

Alexandria lies at the western edge of the Nile river delta. Mark had mentioned this city to me and he told me that it was a great centre of Jewish learning and that the Christians were a growing part of the community there.

By this time Clement had won favour with our master and was in charge of us slaves. He brought me to a meeting of one of the Christian groups and it was there that I met with Jonathan. Jonathan was about two metres in height and with his flowing black hair, enormous eyes and craggy countenance looked more like a seasoned warrior than a gentle Christian. I quickly discerned, however, that his personality was warm and outgoing – a gentle giant.

Jonathan was a Samaritan who became an early disciple of Yeshua following Yeshua's meeting with a woman of their town at Jacob's Well. He told me that he became more and more enchanted with Yeshua as time passed and followed him with his disciples. Until the faithful day.

"*What happened?*" I asked.

"*It was an eventful day. With only a few loaves of bread and some fish he miraculously provided enough food for over five thousand of us - in fact there was loads left over.*"

"*I don't understand*" I said.

"*No. I don't either. It was a miracle. Then he left us and we put out to sea heading back to Capernaum. However, a tremendous storm blew up and we were afraid.*"

"*I can understand that*", I said remembering my voyage to Brindisi.

"*Next thing, what do we see? Yeshua walking on the sea. Walking! We were terrified. Then he reaches the boat and immediately we are docked at Capernaum. It was then that I knew. I knew that he was the Messiah*"

I just stared at him. A human cannot walk on water. Even if he could he couldn't do it through several metres of high waves and a storm force wind. And then suddenly they arrived at their destination. No. Either he is lying or he blacked out and slept and dreamed until they reached port. I realised that my mouth was agape and my eyes were staring and I brought myself to my senses.

Jonathan was smiling. "*I don't blame you for doubting. I could hardly believe my own eyes. But I have the testimony of the disciples who accompanied me on the crossing. However, that was not the most extraordinary thing that occurred on that day.*"

"*Oh? What was that?*" I asked wondering what could be stranger than multiplying loaves of bread out of nothing, walking on water and sailing faster than the speed of thought. Jonathan looked at me intently and asked:

"*Do you believe?*"

"*Believe what?*" I asked somewhat irritably.

"*Do you believe that Yeshua was and is the Son of God and that he rose to life from being dead? Have you heard what took place during the last meal he shared with his disciples?*"

"*No*", I replied being tempted to sarcastically add that I hadn't yet received that "*gift*".

"*Well then, I'm afraid to tell you what occurred later. Yeshua made a claim that caused many who had been following him to turn away from him. Even we who stayed were dumbfounded and unable to understand what this gentle and loving person could mean. It only became clear to us following that last meal with him.*"

I stared at him. My curiosity was aroused. Maybe I was now getting to the crux of what these Christians were up to. Could it be a plot to overthrow Rome, I wondered? What could the Nazarene be claiming? Did he have secret allies in Egypt or Persia? Or in India, perhaps? I had to know. I had to goad him into revealing this matter.

"*So, you are a secret society after all*" I taunted him, "*you posture that you are open to all men but, now I find that that* is not so. You refuse to be open and honest with me. You prevaricate and dissemble. How can you expect me to believe anything that you say?" I realised that Jonathan was gazing at me intently and became aware of how much bigger than me he was. I paused and there followed one of those uneasy silences filled with tension.

Then, and much to my relief, Jonathan smiled.

"*But*", he continued:

"*As the Royal Philosopher has said: there is 'a time to keep silent and a time to speak'. Now is not the time to speak. You are not ready.*"

My relief turned to anger. Who did he think he was? I'm always ready. But, what could I do? I stomped off with as much disdain as I could muster.

Back in the boat I recapitulated to Clement the discussion that I had had with Jonathan. I suppose that I was looking for some moral support from him. I didn't get it – at least, that is what I felt at the time. Clement just smiled and said:

"*Jonathan was right. He discerned that you are not yet ready. You will have to choose. And, you need to be free to be able to choose. You have to be not afraid. And that means that you have to trust.*"

I didn't understand what Clement was saying to me. In my journey through life, and particularly as an investigative reporter, I have learned not to trust anything or anybody unless I can verify a person or event myself. I have to say that I was somewhat miffed with Clement for not supporting me in my exasperation with Jonathan. But, at the same time I respected Clement and, to a certain extent, trusted him.

"*I'll mull it over*", I said and we went for a night's sleep in our hammocks.

The dream

Night has fallen. I sleep. I am in Galilee – how did I get here, I wondered? No matter, the air is balmy. There is a full moon in a cloudless sky. The Sea of Galilee is calm, the waves are tiny and fluttering on to the shore like the wings of pigeons. Peter and James have put to sea. I am in James' boat along with six of Yeshua's disciples. Peter's boat also has a complement of eight. We are trawling a net between our boats. But we were not catching any fish. But that doesn't matter. It is a beautiful peaceful night and I am feeling more relaxed and at peace with myself than I have for a long time.

After a few hours the wind has begun to pick up and the sea has become choppier. "*There is a storm coming*" shouts Peter and we haul in the nets. We set a course for Capernaum. "*What is that?*" shouts one of the men, pointing to the west. "*It is the Lord*" responds Peter and he gets out of his boat and starts walking toward Yeshua. Walking! On the sea!

I am mesmerized. I'm remembering the story told to me by Jonathan. Could this really be happening – again – before my eyes? Then I hear Yeshua's voice calling to me, "*Come to me, Dónal*". I feel very afraid, but incomprehensibly I find myself climbing over the side of the boat and walking toward him. But not before I have secured myself with a rope around my waist and attached to the mast. I needn't be afraid, I think. I am actually walking on the water. Hard to believe. But it is actually happening.

Suddenly I stop. I have reached the end of my rope. I look down and see what I take to be a leviathan. Panic. I begin to sink.

"*Untie the rope*" from James.

"*No way*" from me.

"*Believe*" from Peter.

"*Believe what?*" from me.

"*Let go*".

"*I can't let go*".

I dare not let go of the rope – it is my only hope of being saved. My only hope. And I begin to sink. In my frenzy I remember Clement saying: "*Jonathan was right - you are not ready*".
I try to untie the rope but the water is over my face. The leviathan is coming to me with a huge gaping mouth. My rope is taking me to the leviathan and away from Yeshua. Down, down and I awaken on the floor. Clement is cradling me and singing softly

Here I am, Lord
Is it I, Lord?
I have heard You calling in the night
I will go, Lord
If You lead me

over and over again.
We lay like that for some time, Clement soothing me, and, me eventually becoming calm.
"*It was just a dream*" I said.
"*Not just a dream*", said Clement, "*no ordinary dream. Reminds me of the dreams that Joseph had before marrying Mary. Except it was an angel who appeared to him in his dreams. Who appeared to you? Who gave you an invitation?*"
"*But it was only my imagination*".
"*Listen, Dónal. You have been invited to accept a gift.*"
"*What gift?*" I asked, thinking: there's that word again.
"*Ah Dónal*" sighed Clement. "*The gift of Life. Eternal Life. Look into your deepest self. Who will you follow? Mammon or God? Caesar or Yeshua? Where do you wish to live, in this temporal world or in the Kingdom of God? By the fruit of the tree shall you know which is the good tree. You cannot cling to your old beliefs and have belief in Yeshua. You must let go the rope.*"
I could feel the nurturing goodness flowing to me from Clement, but my mind had stopped working. I was thoroughly exhausted.

"Clement, thank you for your compassion, but I am flummoxed and I need to rest."

"Yes, of course you do Dónal. But continue with your 'mulling".

Nicodemus

Cyprus

Guess who I saw waiting for us as we landed at Kition? Yes, my friend Nicodemus. He brought me and Clement to a villa where we enjoyed a meal with a number of his neighbours. Nicodemus was the host and, again they performed that ceremony with bread and wine with which they always end their meals. Then Nicodemus took me with him to the end of the garden where we sat looking at the crescent moon over the shimmering sea.

"*You have met with my friend, Joseph of Arimathea, haven't you?*"

"*Yes. That seems like another lifetime ago.*"

"*Do you remember what I told you about Yeshua creating bedlam in the Temple during Passover week?*"

"*Yes, I remember very well.*"

"*That seems to have been the last straw for the Chief Priest and his retinue. They captured him and had him tortured and crucified.*"

"*I am aware of that,*" I interrupted him, "*and then he...*"

"*Listen!*" he snapped. "*Unless somebody intervened the body of a crucified person would be removed by the Roman soldiers on duty and hauled to a nearby valley called 'Himnon' where it would be unceremoniously dumped into the pit located there with the rest of the city's trash, then sprinkled with sulphur powder and left to burn and rot. Joseph and I could not countenance such a thing happening with Yeshua's body. Joseph persuaded Pilate to allow him to recover Yeshua's dead body and inter it in a tomb owned by Joseph. Although we were both in dread of the punishment for uncleanness we determined to recover Yeshua's body because of the esteem in which we held him.*"

> Publisher's note.
> A brief note on uncleanness.
> Corpse uncleanness is a state of ritual uncleanness described in Jewish halachic law. It is the highest grade of uncleanness, or defilement, and is contracted by having either directly or indirectly touched, carried or shifted a dead human body.
> A person is required to undergo a seven-day purification period after making physical contact with a human corpse.
> Those persons who were defiled by the dead and who had not yet purified themselves by the ashes of the red heifer followed by immersion in a ritual bath were prohibited from entering the Court of the Israelites (inner court), located on the Temple Mount.
> The impurity that is caused by the dead is considered the ultimate impurity, one which cannot be purified through the waters of an ablution alone (mikvah). Human corpse uncleanness requires an interlude of seven days, accompanied by purification through sprinkling of the ashes of the *Parah Adumah*, the red heifer.
> It will be seen, therefore that the actions of Joseph and Nicodemus would have rendered them unclean and unable to attend Temple ceremonies on the Sabbath of Passover week. It would have brought them into opprobrium with the members of the Sanhedrin and public disgrace in Jerusalem.

"We took his cross out of the ground and laid it flat. Then we had to take out the spikes that were pinning his hands and feet to the wood. The women who had waited beside him since he started his journey from the procurator's palace only had time to give his body a cursory cleansing and anointing with myrrh and spices. Then Joseph and I wrapped his body in linen cloths and brought it to a tomb owned by Joseph and laid it in there. We began to take the great stone wheel with which the tomb would be sealed. Before we could move it, it happened."

He seemed overcome and paused to catch his breath.

I stared, *"what happened?"*

"The scales dropped from our eyes. Suddenly, in the depths of despair and loss, we knew. I looked at Joseph and I could see that he knew. And he looked at me. Joy and wonder crashed in

on our grief. Grief was still there, but, overshadowed by faith, hope and love. In the midst of the turmoil, I think that Joseph actually smiled for an instant. Oh, the happiness I felt. The women who had accompanied us must have thought we had taken leave of our senses."

He paused. I looked at him and could see that he was trembling and transported. I did not have any idea as to what he was talking about. It would have been grim and unsettling experience, so how could he suddenly be happy? Happy? I could only stutter,

"Happiness! Happiness? What was there to be happy about?" I asked.

"Somehow, in the depths of my being I knew that Yeshua would rise from the dead. We had been told that on many occasions he had said that he would rise on the third day after his death. Do you remember how I told you he chased the moneylenders out of the Temple?"

"Yes."

"Well, when he had done that the Jews asked him, 'What sign can you show us for doing this? And he replied, 'Destroy this temple, and in three days I will raise it up'. They thought that he was talking about their great stone Temple. But he was speaking of the temple of his body. That was to be the sign of who he was. And, of course that is what came to pass."

So you say, I thought. At the same time, I was caught up in the ambience of his euphoria. I felt good. I was happy for him. I remembered Joseph going on ecstatically in the same way. And I found myself wishing I could have some of that peacefulness and certitude. And the little interior voice started again with, is it possible?...you could...why don't you?...take courage...let go, let God...seize the moment...be not afraid...

We sat quietly for a while as he became calm.

"It was some kind of miracle you know", he said, "in an instant all that I had heard about him and all he had said to me became clear and meaningful."

"*How do you mean?*" I asked.

"*We knew in our deepest hearts that Yeshua was our God in human form. No, not 'was', he 'is'. The Messiah is a much greater being than anything the prophets had foretold. Yahweh has become flesh and dwells among us. And we have been privileged to meet him.*"

I simply didn't know what to make of this. But he was a nice man and I didn't want to offend him. I was wondering what on earth he and Joseph were doing there anyway. Hadn't the Sanhedrin, of which he and Joseph were members, orchestrated this outcome? And, where were Yeshua's disciples? Presumably some other Jewish elders and, probably, Herodians would have been there to ensure that the threat to their status was eradicated? How would they have regarded the actions by Nicodemus and Joseph – not only showing association with a person who had been a blasphemer and a plotter seeking to be king - but, also performing tasks so far beneath their dignity?

"*We rolled a great stone against the door of the tomb and went away. We spent the Sabbath thanking God for what he had done for us and on the first day of the week Yeshua rose from the dead and met with many of his disciples then and over the following weeks. It was also the first day of a new world, the Christian world. I was reminded of the first day of creation when God said 'Let there be light'. We now have the light of the world and have been instructed to*

'Go therefore and make disciples of all nations, baptizing them in the name of the Father and of the Son and of the Holy Spirit, and teaching them to obey everything I have commanded you. And remember, I am with you always to the end of the age.'"

"*But he is not with us any longer*", I protested. "*Didn't he ascend into the sky never to be seen again?*"

"*It is good that you ask questions. I think that you are now ready to hear what Jonathan hesitated to tell you.*"

"*What is that?*" I enquired.

To my annoyance he replied: "*You must ask Jonathan the next time you meet him.*"

And, that was that. It was time to return to our ship.

A Gift?

One thing that Clement has in abundance is patience. He never asked me anything about my conversation with Nicodemus. After two days and following our evening meal I recounted what Nicodemus had told me. He nodded every now and then as I spoke.
"*What do you think?*" I asked.
"*Nicodemus is a good man. He and Joseph always sought the truth. Even as he died Yeshua gave them the grace to believe that Yeshua was indeed the Son of God sent to redeem us from sin and that not even death could separate us from him. Nicodemus knew with absolute certainty that Yeshua would defeat death and that, as he had said, would be with us always.*"
This was extremely frustrating. Even if one were to accept that somehow, he became alive again, didn't he disappear shortly afterwards? So, how could he still be with us? And there is Nicodemus burying him and he suddenly believes in him. How could that be? One would think that Nicodemus would have thought something like, "*Well, that's that. All has come to naught. It is over. He couldn't have been Divine because the Divine can't die. Maybe this is God's way of punishing him for claiming to be the Son of God. A bit of Sodom and Gomorrah treatment. A pity since he seemed to be such a good man. But, good or not, if you go around saying that you are God when you're not, as is obvious by his death, then you suffer the consequences.*"
But Nicodemus didn't think that. And Yeshua is believed to have become alive shortly afterwards, but differently alive. Is that actually true? How could it be? I suppose that if it is true then his death wasn't a punishment by God. So, why would God let himself be tortured and killed? Back to my touchstone question: "*Cui bono?*" – "*Who profits?*". I can't see that anybody gets anything out of his death and resurrection. And, if he

were this all-powerful being why wouldn't he wreak havoc amongst all involved in his torture and execution? I can't think of anybody who wouldn't do so in such circumstances. Are we really supposed to believe that, just before he died, he said, "*Father, forgive them for they know not what they do.*" I try to picture myself being falsely convicted, tortured and crucified to death. And my oppressors standing around gloating and taunting me – well, I can tell you that if somehow I became alive some time afterward I would make it my life's work to annihilate those wretches. And, I would enjoy doing it.

"*Easy there Dónal, shalom, shalom*" from Clement as he laid a hand on my shoulder.

With a start I realised that my fists were clenched and my face was somewhat contorted.

"*Sorry*", I said, "*while I don't believe what you Christians believe I am appalled at the awful injustice of what was done. Those miscreants should not be allowed to get away with their malicious atrocity.*"

I was still seething with rage at the injustice of it all.

"*I just don't get you Christians. You believe that God became a man, was killed, became alive again and then disappeared shortly afterwards. What was the point? What was achieved? Nothing. Yeshua just created a bit of aggravation in a remote country for a few years. Then he was gone and the world carries on in the same old way.*"

We sat in silence for several minutes. Clement, eyes closed, was nodding and I was slowly regaining some composure. Eventually Clement broke the silence with,

"*Ecclesiastes says that*

*'For everything there is a season
and a time for every matter under heaven:
a time to be born and a time to die;
a time to plant and a time to pluck up what is planted'*

and the list goes on. I believe that, in His infinite wisdom, God decides the time at which you will receive from Him in a flow of grace the gift of Faith".

I looked at him. My blood was rising. There it was again – this "*gift*" thing. It was so frustrating. Like a magician's "*abracadabra*". Why would I supposedly need some kind of gift to understand? I was reasonably intelligent. And I was open-minded. If something made sense I could understand it – I didn't need a gift to understand it – I already had a gift – it is called "reason".

"*What do I have to do to earn this gift?*"

"*Nothing*".

"*Nothing?*" I snapped.

"*You cannot do anything to earn or deserve it. It is a gift.*"

"*Enough*!" I shouted and stomped away.

Jonathan.
Alexandria
(And a portal to another world).

It was many months before our boat, the Dreamy Drifter, again berthed at Alexandria. During those days I mused over my various encounters with the Christians. I found myself comparing them with my non-Christian acquaintances. I realised that I preferred being in their company. Somewhat strangely these Christians seemed to be more purposeful. And my mind strayed to my encounter with the slave Theo. Was he a stupid servile nonentity or...or what? His demeanour may have been somewhat self-effacing but there was also a purposefulness in him – in a contradictory way he seemed to be "*his own man*". Yes, that was it, they were all self-assured, but not in any arrogant or highhanded manner. It was as though they knew something very important of which the rest of us were unaware. They seemed to be more at peace with the world.
It couldn't be the existence of something other than this world which all of us sense – could it? If so, where could it be? And, if we couldn't sense it, why did it matter anyway? And even if what they said was true, living in what they called "*a Christian lifestyle*" would be too inhibiting for me to contemplate. "*Nothing to do with me*" I thought.
I did, however, like their idea of one all-powerful God – the prime mover as the Greek philosophers described him. Okay, so he set this whole universe in motion. Why would he care what happened to us paltry humans after that? Probably off on some other more gratifying projects.
Such was my mindset in those days. Looking back, I can see that I was in denial. I was holding on to that "*rope*" I had depended on in my dream. That was my mental state and I am amused to note that in my physical state I was also in the denial in the Nile. The Nile delta measures 20,000 square

kilometres and contains 144 islands – a busy place! That gives a good picture of what my mental state was at that time.

We spent a little over two days unloading from the ship what we had brought and reloading it with goods destined for sale elsewhere. On the third day, although quite tired, Clement and I went to Jonathan's villa for an evening meal. Jonathan drew me aside afterwards.

"*Clement tells me that you may be ready to hear the rest of what I would like to say to you*", he said.

Well, in fact I was quite tired and dozy after the meal and what I wanted to do was curl up and have a good sleep. But I couldn't be ungracious with my host.

"Oh yes".

"*On the night before he was crucified Yeshua celebrated a Passover meal with his disciples. As you may know a Passover meal is to celebrate the miraculous escape from Egypt and a new beginning for the Jews. It was at that meal that Yeshua brought to fruition something he had talked about earlier. Taking bread he blessed the bread, broke the bread and gave the bread to his followers saying, 'Take, eat; this is my body, which is given for you. Do this in remembrance of me'".*

Jonathan paused. I was trying to absorb what he was saying. I was having difficulty making sense of it.

"*He said that bread was his body?*" I asked.

"Yes".

"*The bread that he was holding in his hands?*"

"Yes".

I was now fully awake. Wondering if Jonathan was insane.

"*And he broke it and gave it to the others?*"

"Yes."

"*And then, what?*"

"They ate it."

"*They ate the bread which he said was his body? As if they were eating his body?*"

"Yes".

I stared at Jonathan for a long while. He didn't seem to be insane although he had a kind of gentle smile. So, Yeshua says that some bread is his body and his disciples eat it. Well, I suppose that is possible. I mean if someone gave me some bread and said "*This is venison*" I could eat it, but I would know that it was still bread regardless of what someone called it.

"*So, he was giving them some kind of symbolism? The bread symbolised his body and their eating it symbolised a deep connection between them. Is that it? So that, after he was killed, which he seemed to know was going to happen imminently, this would be a way to remember him? Okay, I think I get it. You had me nervous for a while.*"

There was a silence for some moments while Jonathan looked at me intently and I think that I was holding my breath.

"*No.*"

"*'No' what?*" I asked wishing that I had kept my mouth shut. But the reporter's curiosity had taken over – get to the nub of the matter.

"*It wasn't symbolic it was actual.*"

"*What do you mean?*"

"*The bread was no longer bread, it was Yeshua. Each piece of what appeared to be bread in the hands of the disciples was Yeshua.*"

My head was reeling. This was crazy talk. There could be only one Yeshua and he was sitting at the table. How could there be several other Yeshuas in the hands of his fellow diners? I could feel my temper rising listening to this, as it then appeared to me, nonsensical gibberish. Did Jonathan take me for a total idiot?

"*That is enough, Jonathan. What you are saying is self-contradictory and irrational even if you cannot see it that way. I'm leaving. Thank you for a nice meal. I know that you do not mean me any harm and will I leave you to your delusions. They are not for me. Vale.*"

I must have raised my voice somewhat for Clement had heard me and had come over to join us.

"*I'm going back to the ship, Clement. This man is not right in his head.*"

"*I know that it is a bit of a thunderbolt. Just listen for a while and we will put it in context.*"

I gaped at him in horror. "*Don't tell me that you too believe this...this...this gibberish? Are all you Christians into this? We're beyond talking about things like square circles here, we're into the world of lunacy, some kind of mad necromancers. I am deeply offended that you people expect me to believe something so outrageous. I've had it with the lot of you.*"

Turning on my heel I left them and headed back to the ship. Clement followed me and I quickened my pace. I had already lost my body to a slave owner – I wasn't about to lose my mind to these crazy Christians no matter how congenial they were. I got into my hammock before Clement could catch up with me and, eyes closed, ignored him. Clement respected my silence.

I knew that I had had some very disturbing dreams that night, but, when I woke up, I couldn't remember any details. I woke up tired and moody. Alone and morose. Avoiding eye contact with Clement – giving him the cold shoulder.

At sea again.

That morning, we put to sea heading for Sidon, some 600 kilometres away. It was a pleasant journey and the repetitive tasks helped to take my mind off the harrowing bewilderment caused by Jonathan's preposterous figment.

On the third day at sea the weather changed suddenly. The sun was blotted out by heavy black stygian clouds. The darkness was broken by continuous vicious spears of lightning. The thunder was deafening. The wind convulsed back and forth like a demented demon. And the sea retaliated with waves rising to as much as thirty metres which pummelled our boat relentlessly. A shaft of lightning shattered our mainmast. A vicious current swept our rudders away. Implacable waves assaulted the boat mercilessly. The enfeebled boat capitulated, broke up and descended to a watery grave leaving its crew at the mercy of the elements. There was no mercy. Or, so I thought. I was clinging to some flotsam feeling very sorry for myself and in abject fear of my impending death. Waves hammered my body relentlessly seemingly determined to separate me from...

And then I laughed. Delirium was setting in. I could hardly believe it -the life-saving flotsam was in the shape of a cross. *"Ha, ha, ha, am I also to die on a cross, Yeshua?"* I cried. Is this some kind of divine joke? Is Neptune punishing me for listening to those Christians who say he doesn't exist. I don't care. I don't care if it is Neptune or Yeshua or any god. None are around when they are needed. They don't care about me and I don't care about them. Do you think your trial was unfair, Yeshua? Well, I didn't even get a trial. So, if either of you exists you are unjust and I defy you. I defy you, do you hear? *"What have I done to be visited with so much misfortune? Abduction and imprisonment. Slavery and gruelling manual labour. And now a horrible protracted dying."*

Mercifully the palliative of unconsciousness approached. I relaxed. The sea wrenched at my cross and I let go. Sinking. "*No, no. Oh God, no. Please. No, no, no.*" I was sinking into the swirling silence below the maelstrom and into blissful nothingness. No flotsam cross, no rope, no hope. Nothing. Gone.

Hope...maybe!

What? What? Not gone? Something. What? Feeling. Am I on the ground? I can't see. Is this what it is like to be dead? Am I disembodied? No, I feel the ground. But I can't move, can't see. But I can hear something. Faintly.
"*Oh. Al. Oh, al.*" The noise seems to be coming from far away. There it is again. "*Oh. Al. Oh, al.*" Suddenly I know that sound and I try to smile and there it is more distinctly:
"*Dónal, Dónal*", so softly.
That is Clement, I'm sure it is. I feel a hand on my shoulder. My blood quickens. I am trembling. Am I still alive? Is that even possible? My eyes open and flutter and I can dimly see an expanse of blue sky. Then I see Clement's smiling face above me. I must be alive. Or, is he dead also?
"*Welcome back, Dónal*".
"*Ha, ha, ha,*" I can't help it. I am overcome with a fit of childish giggles. Clement is laughing too as he caresses my head.
"*You need to rest for a while*" he says. That sets off another bout of helpless laughing which peters out with me falling into a deep sleep.
I don't know how long I slept. But when I awoke it was dark and Clement had a fire crackling in a ring of stones. I sat up. Ouch, every bit of my body ached and complained. I didn't care – I wasn't dead. He handed me a bowl of water which I gulped down. Then, miraculously as far as I was concerned, some food and more water. As I wolfed down the food, which seemed more delicious than anything I had ever eaten in my life, I asked him:
"*Where did you get this?*"
"*Don't you know that God provides?*" He smiled, "*actually there is a stream nearby and some stuff washed ashore from the boat.*"
"*Don't talk to me about your God*" I said, "*where was he when that storm assaulted us?*"

Silence.

The silence continued so that, after a while, I interrupted my greedy gobbling to look up at him. I couldn't make out what his look was meant to convey.

"*What?*"

"*Oh, Dónal, Dónal. In a similar storm Yeshua rebuked the wind and said to the sea, 'Be silent! Be still!' Then the wind ceased, and there was a dead calm. He said to his disciples, 'Why are you afraid? Have you still no faith?'*

Are you not alive, Dónal? And on dry land? And with food and water? How did you get from breathing your last beneath the water to resting on dry land alive? Have you still no faith?"

I gaped at him. What was he implying, I wondered. Is he trying to get me to believe that his God somehow rescued me? As if reading my thoughts Clement asked:

"*Is it possible?*"

"*No!*" I blurted.

"*Is it possible?*"

"*No.*" again.

"*So, you say that it is not possible. Not only that it didn't happen, but, that it is impossible that such a thing could happen?*"

Oops! That triggered a vague memory. What was it? Oh yes, that mountebank Aaron Becus with his possible and impossible. Was I equivocating like him?

Me, the dedicated unswerving seeker of truth? Perhaps I need to examine the attitude I brought to conversations with these Christians. Surely, I have an open mind? As I thought about it several possibilities came into my mind. Most if not all of my previous investigations had been to expose the ulterior motives of certain persons or cliques. I had become accustomed to finding that we live in a world of lies and cover-ups. I had dismissed what the Christians said (and, of course, what they said had been quite paradoxical) without giving it much thought – I was looking for juicier stuff. Headline grabbers.

Clement, who I realised had been patiently watching me, interrupted my line of thought.

"*Think of your conversation with Rubin. Think of who you think our God is and who you are. Just God and just you. Nothing else. Nobody else. Who is the essential Dónal? Dónal and God. God and Dónal. I am going to sleep now. We will talk again in the morning. May the Holy Spirit rest with you tonight as you sleep.*"

And he was gone. I threw my mind back and recalled my musings following my talk with Rubin:

One God,

My father,

Cares for me.

ME!

What if that were true? Is it possible? If it were true how wonderful that would be. I began to feel happy.

[Looking back, I can now see that it was at this point that Satan, anxious not to lose one of his serfs, intervened. And, of course Satan hates that anybody should be happy or at peace.]

But, what kind of father who is supposed to be all powerful and full of love would permit his son to be abducted by scoundrels, enslaved and nearly killed in a storm? So, even if there is only one all-powerful God, he has not been like a father to me (there's "*me*" again). He seems more like the lesser God "*who couldn't care less*" described by those Gnostics in Monte Cassino. Somehow (grace?) I caught myself and realised that I was wallowing in self-pity – "*Why me? Poor me. It's not fair*". I didn't like to think of myself being such a wuss.

So, I tried to turn my thinking around, to see positives. It was difficult because the "*poor me*" and entitlement syndromes kept surfacing. Then I realised that fundamentally all of my thinking was built on the proposition that I was the centre of the universe, I was the most important thing that existed for me. On the other hand, if there were such a being as an omnipotent pre-existing creating God wouldn't that God be the centre of the universe? I found myself beginning to smile. There are millions of us humans on this Earth. Does each one think that he or she is the centre of the universe? If so, then there are millions of very small universes. But at least I have to say this much for these Christians. None of them seems to think that he or she is the centre of the universe. At the same time each of them thinks that he or she is super-important – but, then again they think other persons are equally super-important: "*love thy neighbour as thyself*". Well, I could do that, sort of. The problem was that Yeshua's concept of neighbour was a bit too indiscriminate for me – there was no way that I could even like the thugs who had kidnapped me, or forgive them. Yet, Yeshua seemed to have talked a lot about forgiving, even in his last breath. I can't do that kind of thing. Although, wait a minute, I have free will. So, in principle I could forgive them, couldn't I? But, I sure as hell won't. Why should I? Just because Yeshua says so? No, I actually like hating them. And, if there was a God who was an all-powerful and loving father would he forgive humans who did such things to his children? The whole thing was self-contradictory. I'll do my own thing, thank you. Here I am with this "*me*" stuff again. Round and round my mind raced wondering if I might be in a mental *cul-de-sac*. "*But this – but that*" on and on until I drifted off to sleep. What a wonderful blessing sleep can be. I slept deeply that night.

Truth...maybe!

I awoke as dawn broke. It felt so good to wake up as a free man, even though I was lost and owned nothing except the rags I stood in. I stood up and breathed in the sweet sea air. I smiled to myself – it was longer than I could remember that I had felt this good. I turned around to find Clement regarding me with a smile and a raised eyebrow.
"*Bonum mane, Dónal*".
"*Salve, Clement*".
"*We must be on our way. I believe that we are not far from Kition and can reach the city shortly after midday*" he said handing me a leather-skin of water.
I was taken aback. I wanted to stay here. I definitely wanted to stay here. I didn't want to go back to so-called civilisation. I was free here – back there I would be a slave once again. So, I told him that.
"*That is not possible, Dónal. There is no food here, no protection from the elements. Our friends will be worried about us.*"
"*There are fish and there are birds and probably small animals inland. We could build a shelter or, perhaps, find a cave. We could live here in peace. And I don't have any friends to worry about me. I'm just an ordinary human being. I don't have the kind of spiritual experiences that you seem to have.*"
Clement gazed at me. "*Perhaps you have things the wrong way round? I am not a human being having a spiritual experience. We are spiritual beings having a human experience*[7]. *But perhaps it is good for you to be alone with God and nature for a time. I shall call you in time to come. I have a task for you. Sit Deus vobiscum.*"
With that he turned and left. I watched until he disappeared from sight - he did not look back.

---

[7] Pierre Teilhard de Chardin

I was alone but for the sun beating down, waves breaking on the shore, palm leaves rustling in a gentle breeze and the occasional trill of a bird. I sat on the beach gazing at the sea. I sat there for hours with not a care in the world, lulled into a half sleep by the sun and the rhythmic sound of the waves. Musing on my life and thanking God for rescuing me from slavery and the storm. Dozing.

Too hot. I awoke with a start and made my way to the stream that Clement had mentioned, slaked my thirst, doused my overheated body and retreated to the cover of the trees. Wait a moment, I thought. What had I been doing thanking a God I didn't believe in? Had I become delirious in the heat? Or, was I blocking something? Was I tethered by some kind of rope? And now I was on my knees. "*Help me*" I cried to I knew not who or what. "*Please.*" Nothing. "*Give me a sign*". Nothing. "*Give me the gift that those Christians are always talking about.*" Nothing. I fell back and lay on the ground staring at the sky through the fluttering tree tops. Back and forth they went showing one bit of sky and then another bit. Like me, I thought. Am I vacillating? What, me? No, I don't flinch from the truth – I am a fearless reporter shining a light on the truth. Fearless? Am I fearless, I asked myself. And, I tried to say, "*yes*" but found that I couldn't. But, how could I accept this non-physical stuff and paradoxes that the Christians go on about? On the other hand, they didn't seem to be afraid. On the contrary, they seemed to be happy and at peace. And pictures of the ones that I had met came into my head, the slave Theo and his noble bearing, Mary at Magdala and her music and dancing heart, Clement and his compassion, and Nicodemus. And they all cared about me – not for anything they could get from me – just for my wellbeing. And I seemed to hear all of them imploring me: "*Let go, let God*".

And, with some shock, I realised that I was weeping and muttering to myself. "*Let go, let go let go. Do not be afraid, only believe.*"

"*I'm not afraid. I'm not afraid. I'm not* afraid ". I screamed. But of course I was afraid. Even shouting it again and again didn't convince me. It seemed to me that it was as if I was blindfolded and somebody was asking me to take a step into I didn't know what. How could I? And then I thought about the Christians who were asking me to take this step. And I wanted to take that step. "*I can't, I can't, I can't,*" I screamed at the sky. Oh, where was that wonderful feeling of peace that I was enjoying a short while ago on the beach. Gone. My mind was in turmoil once more. And I was thirsty. And fed up with this constant squabble going on in my head.

I got up, went to my stream, slaked my thirst and lay in the water for a while. Ah, that's better, I feel like myself again. I walked down to the sea and paddled looking out at the seemingly endless ocean and listening to the sounds of the waves rolling towards me and lapping around my feet. It was impossible to imagine how this tranquil beautiful body of water could suddenly turn into a malevolent callous murderous monster. And, as I thought about the storm which had nearly claimed my life it had been hard, as I sank, to believe that it could revert to a tranquil scene such as that now before my eyes. But of course I do believe that it can do so because I have experienced the mutation. Aware of that Christian thing trying to get into my head again I said to myself somewhat self-indulgently, "*I believe what I experience*". How could I believe something that I can't experience? And please don't insult my intelligence by telling me that it is a gift.

My mind drifted,

    Mary at Magdala, "*I ask you to join with us in the dance filled with the music of love*",

    Joseph, "*if you have faith in God consider what you might win*",

    Theo with his noble bearing and serene calmness,

    Rubin, "*God is your Abba, you are his beloved son*",

    Clement, "*Nicodemus will offer you the gift*",

Me in my dream with that rope preventing me from leaving the boat, a boat which in a storm betrayed me and left me helpless against the elements,
a rope which constrained me from...from what?
Jonathan and his bread. Bread?

And compare them with Sorcastic and Aaron Becus.

Then it hit me. The heart and the head. Not the heart beating in my chest, but, something much deeper in my very being. I realised that I was living in my head. And, what is wrong with that, I thought – I'm not some kind of emotional pussycat. But, but, but. My real heart is deeper within me than that. In my heart I want there to be an almighty loving God, a God who loves me and watches over me every minute as a father, as my abba. Oh, I want that. If there is such a God who created me out of love then how can I know? Theo says that he can do one thing, and one thing only, that this God cannot do. And that is to freely and joyously love God. Is that a desire on the part of God which caused him to give me free will? Is the reason that I have free will to love him for having given me lifeness just as his love for the idea of me caused him to create me? I was now deep in my heart and my body rejoiced with tears.

"*I want to believe. Give me the gift, God. Then I will believe.*"
And it seemed that a voice within me said to me, "*you have the gift. You have always had the gift. It is just that You never unwrapped it. Be courageous and cast off the rope. Let go of this world. Let go. Trust God your father who created you so that you could freely love him and there you will find peace, a peace that surpasses all understanding. Trust God as he has trusted you. Surrender your self to God and he will catch you. God is a loving Abba and will gather you as a hen gathers her chickens under her wings. Let go and fly. Fly.*"
"*I want to. I want to.*"
Then, seemingly from nowhere:
"*I do. I do.*"
And I collapsed onto the ground exhausted.

"*I do, oh I do.*"

And the sea continued to caress the shore as it had done for aeons, and the sun sank to rest, supplanted by its nightly sister, the Moon enveloped in the jewellery of the stars and I slept.

I woke up as the sun appeared above the horizon. I lay there for a while listening to the sea and the chatter of the birds and feeling at peace. And...and...happy. Happy?

I marvelled at how I had not seen the truth of my existence for so many years. But now there was so much to learn. Had my Father put me here for a reason, I wondered? Had I always been asking myself that question in some indistinct way? Was that why I became a reporter? Tell me, Lord.

We are all the product of our circumstances. And I thought of Theo and smiled. "*It is the will of God who loves me*". There is the flesh and the spirit. For all of my life I had conducted my living in the service of the flesh. Now I was released from that bondage. Or at least I knew it was there and could aspire to something infinitely more self-fulfilling than "*eat, drink and be merry*" and knew that "*tomorrow we die*" was infinitely far from the truth.

There was something that I needed to do. I needed to be baptised into the spirits of the Christians I had met and into the spirit of Yeshua. Then I must find a mission. Something to try and make up for the damage I had done to Yeshua's followers. For a start I will get Rumor del Mundi to print my journal. That should be easy enough. What then? Time to consult Clement and Nicodemus.

Truth. New life.

I went to the stream and drank. Then I knelt and tried to pray to God whom I had found. No, I thought, it was God who found me and opened the eyes of my heart. But I couldn't pray – I didn't know how to pray. So, I just said, "*thank you, thank you*" on and on. It didn't seem enough and so I apologised for not being much good at praying. And I promised that I would learn from the Christians. I wondered if they would let me join them. I wanted to. So, I asked my newly found Abba if he would help in the matter…was that a prayer, I wondered. I had a lot to learn.

I stood up and headed for Kition in the footsteps of Clement. Good footsteps to follow, I thought with a smile. I was so hungry. Oh, oh! On cue the devil suggested to me that hunger was the real reason behind my journey to Kition. But I now had a protector, "*God, God, God*" I murmured and that worked.

A short distance from Kition there was Nicodemus coming to meet me, his arms outstretched like the father in the parable of the prodigal son – yes, I had listened during those suppers with the Christians.

He enveloped me in a great hug. "*Dónal, Dónal, I am so glad to see you. I knew that you would be coming.*"

"*Well, I…*" I started.

"*I know. I know. I can see it plainly in your eyes.*" He stopped hugging, stepped back, grabbed my arm, and, with a big smile, said, "*As our Lord and Master would say, follow me.*"

He led me to Kition, then through some streets to a compound. We entered a room to find Clement and some other Christians to whom I was introduced and who greeted me with "*pax vobiscum*". Clement came and put an outstretched hand on my shoulder. And, with a most serious face looked deeply into my eyes, "*I know what you need*" he said solemnly. I trembled. Then, with a broad smile he turned and pointed to the table saying "*porridge and bread*". And there was a big bowl of porridge and loaves. I sat and ate ravenously to the amusement of all.

In the following days I had discussions with Clement and Nicodemus and the others who told me of the life and teachings and mission of Yeshua. They brought together all I had heard from Peter, Paul, Mark, Matthew and so many others at suppers I had attended. On the third day I said that I wished to be baptized. They demurred saying that prayer was needed. I was to contemplate deeply the life and Faith that I wished to embrace.

I did so and, in my reporter's methodical way, made a list:
- There is only one God who is love and who existed before anything else;
- But, somehow, there are three persons in this one God;
- God created space, time and the universe;
- God became a human through a virgin named Mary who remained a virgin.
- That human, Yeshua, had the natures of a human and of God;
- Yeshua lived an "ordinary" everyday life for 30 years in an obscure village;
- Yeshua then spent about three years forgiving sins, exorcising demons, performing miraculous cures and teaching Truth;
- Yeshua was tortured and murdered;
- Yeshua died;
- Of his own power that divine person became alive again;
- Then Yeshua left the Earth-as-sensed -by-humans after a short time;
- Yeshua sent the Advocate to guide and protect Yeshua's followers in the Truth;
- Followers of Yeshua share meals where they consume bread and wine as spiritual food and sustenance;

- God in the person of the Holy Spirit presides over the followers of Yeshua to keep their beliefs True.
- We await the coming of God's Kingdom (which is "*near*") to Earth.
- We are to take up our "*cross*" every day and follow Yeshua who is the "*way, the truth and the life*".

I showed my list to Nicodemus. He read it and smiled.
"*Are you ready to love God with all of your heart and your neighbour as yourself?*" he asked.
"*Yes*" I said feeling full of joy.
"*Does that include the Romans who captured you at Frosinone, imprisoned you in the Mamertine, and the ruffians who purchased you from them and sold you to a slave owner and the slave owner?*" he asked.
"*What?*", How could I possibly like those bad persons. I was stunned and speechless.
"*Well?*" from Nicodemus.
"*How could I possibly like such scoundrels after what they did to me and others. Including Clement. Does Clement like them? I just can't do that.*"
Nicodemus smiled, "*I'm not asking you if you like them*", he said.
I blinked. "*What do you mean?*" I asked.
"*To love is not the same as to like. You can like all kinds of things without loving them, oranges, swimming, sculpting. Liking is something appealing to part of one's physical self. You can love without liking.*
Think of the good Samaritan caring for the injured man from Jerusalem – he didn't necessarily like his patient, but he clearly loved him. Think of Stephen. I'm sure that he didn't like the people stoning him to death, but there is no doubt that he loved them. As they stoned him, he knelt down and cried out in a loud voice, 'Lord, do not hold this sin against them.' When he had said this, he died."

Well, I had never made that distinction before. Now, I was confused: what did I like but not love; was there anything or anybody that I loved but did not like; was there anything or anybody that I liked and loved? The last one was easy: Yeshua. Nicodemus interrupted my thoughts, "*Liking has to do with this world and can be good, for example, liking wine, or bad, for example, liking too much wine. Loving has to do with the heart and God's world.*

Yeshua enjoined us to 'Love our enemies and pray for those who persecute us'. Is not each one of those who wronged you a child of God? Satan had entered their hearts and led them astray. Are they not to be pitied rather than hated for the dreadful things that they did? Can you pray for them? Can you ask God to rescue them from Satan's sway? That would be loving them while not loving their bad deeds.

On the evening of the first day when he rose from the dead the first thing that Yeshua said to the apostles was:

'Peace be with you. As the Father has sent me, so I send you.' When he had said this, he breathed on them and said to them, 'Receive the Holy Spirit. If you forgive the sins of any, they are forgiven them; if you retain the sins of any, they are retained.' The message from the glorified Christ was to be at peace and he gave his apostles the Divine power to forgive sins. God had been forgiving us again and again since the fall of our first parents. But, from that time we humans have not been forgiving.

Now, I want you to spend some time in praying to Yeshua about love and asking him for discernment. When you think that you are ready come to me. One question that I shall ask you is whether or not you forgive all of those who have done wrong things to you. Strangely enough that might include forgiving God. It also will probably involve forgiving yourself."

Then he beckoned a young man named Timothy.

"*Timothy will take you to a mountain called Terra Oliva which is about forty kilometres away. He will leave you there with provisions for several days. You know that it was the habit of Yeshua to go to a mountain to pray. We ask you to pray for guidance and return to us in several days. May God go with you."*

So, we made the trek to the mountain. Timothy led me to the top where there was a rough shack that was to serve as my shelter and left me.

Alone again.

Soul searching.

It had been noon by the time that we had reached the hut, the start of the *Hours of Common Silence* in Cyprus and time for a *riposo*. So, when Timothy departed, I rested but I couldn't sleep. My mind fluttered …love…Yeshua…cross…forgive…repent…gift…faith…me. Eventually I did fall asleep for a few hours. When I awoke my first thought was "*me*". Why should I forgive those thugs who had ruined my life? If I was to follow Yeshua did I have to love them? How could I? Then it occurred to me, what difference would it make to them whether or not I forgave them? None. None! What difference would it make for me? None. None??? How did I know that? Wasn't the history of the Jewish people saturated with instances of God forgiving them. Yes, except they hadn't beaten God or sold God into slavery like those thugs did to me. Making a golden statue in the form of a calf and then adoring it as a god seemed to me to be utterly stupid rather than a bad thing to do. Although turning their backs on God after all he had done for them and saying that their delivery from slavery was down to a calf was mind-bogglingly insulting.

Oh, oh, here I was trying to find excuses not to forgive. And I remembered what Yeshua prayed as he hung dying, "*…for they know not what they do*". But those thugs knew what they were doing to me. Or, did they? I had to admit to myself that it wasn't personal – I was simply a commodity. My bad luck to be where I was when they struck. Then I recalled that the only thing I was enjoined to do in the prayer given to us by Yeshua was:

> *as we forgive*
> *those who trespass against us,*
> *forgive*
> *us our trespasses*

Oh! So, God is to grant me forgiveness in the same way that I grant forgiveness to other persons.

I had to acknowledge that I had trespassed against God on many occasions. In many ways my sins were as idiotic as worshipping a golden calf. Then my mind wandered to those weekends in Pompeii. I could say that I "*didn't know*" what I did to those women. That was because for me each was a commodity. I didn't let myself think about it. So, I didn't have any idea of what damage I might have done to them and their families. I didn't give such matters a thought at the time – but now it was getting to me. Each of them could address God as Abba in the same way that I could. We were brother and sisters. I had misused Abba's child while Abba looked on. How could God forgive me? Because I "*didn't know*" what I did? Perhaps. But, and it was a "*but*", that as Yeshua had made very clear for me, only "*as I forgave those who trespassed against me*", namely those thugs. And, what did it cost me to forgive them? Nothing. So, why was it so hard?

And then it hit me. It was because for me:

I am the centre of the world.

My goodness! I never realised at any conscious level that everything I had ever thought or ever did emanated from that state of mind – right from the moment of my birth in 28 C.E. And then my thought was "*What about 26 C.E.?*" I didn't exist then – the world had been around for thousands of years – I wasn't even an idea in anyone's mind. Or, maybe I was an idea in God's mind – isn't He omniscient? And, suddenly I came into existence. I didn't bring me into existence. Did my parents? Did they create me as a being having lifeness and personal identification? Yes, they were involved in the matter. But did they simply build this body with sensory organs to accommodate my spirit? Or, was it to accommodate my soul? No, "*accommodate*" is not the right word. I am not just my body, not just my soul, not just my spirit – I am me. I am a human being. My "I" is also spiritual. But isn't the spiritual ingredient superior to the physical ingredient? I tend to think of myself as a human being having a spiritual experience. Could it be the other way round? Am I, as Clement remarked, actually a spiritual being having a human experience?[8]

No! I am me. A spirited body, an embodied spirit – "*the Lord God formed man from the dust of the ground and breathed into his nostrils the breath of life, and the man became a living being*".[9] The dust was enlivened.

Nowadays it is a woman and man who form the body but it still God who breaths human lifeness into the body.

When I speak of "*my body*" or "*my soul*" or "*my spirit*" I am asserting the pre-eminence of me over my body, and over my soul and over my spirit. I am something greater than body, soul and spirit – I am me.

I paused. What does all that mean? Firstly, I know that I am not the centre of the universe. That is a good start Dónal, I said to myself. God is the centre of the universe. Now we are getting places Dónal, I said to myself. His Son became a human to tell and show us how to live in a way that is pleasing to God – and, of course, that is good for us. Is this what he meant when he said, "*The time is fulfilled and the kingdom of God has come near*"?

I was beginning to fall asleep, but feeling that for the future I could live a good life if I kept in mind the two greatest commandments: love God all the time with all my heart and love everyone else as much as myself. But what was this "*take up your cross daily...*" thing?

Help me, Yeshua.

Sleep.

---

[8] Teilhard de Chardin.
[9] Genesis 2:7

Bread, manna, new bread.

In the morning, I was roused from sleep by, of all people, Jonathan of Alexandria.

"Forgive me for disturbing you", he said, *"I have brought some food for our breakfast"*, pointing to the table.

As I rose, I smiled that his first word to me was "*forgive*" and saw that he was also smiling.

"All right, Jonathan. It is good to see you again. Are you here to tell me what you were afraid to relate in Alexandria? Do you imagine that anything could now make me turn away from Yeshua?"

We sat down to breakfast.

"First of all, let me tell you something else. In the storm which wrecked the Dreamy Drifter your master perished. And all of his records also disappeared. So, there is no record of you being a slave. You and Clement are free men to go about your lives as you please."

Well, that was great news and I felt that a weight was lifted from me. We went outside and sat looking over the valleys to the sea as the sun started on its daily pilgrimage to the western horizon.

"But, come, tell me about this amazing event," I said.

"You recall my telling you of the feeding of the five thousand with five loaves, Yeshua walking on the sea and us suddenly reaching Capernaum?"

"Yes."

"When the crowd discovered that Yeshua was not on their side of the sea they made their way to Capernaum and found him with us. Yeshua knew that they sought him because they had been fed by him. He said to them,

'Do not work for the food that perishes but for the food that endures for eternal life, which the Son of Man will give you.'

And they said to him,

'give us a sign to show us who you are. Our ancestors ate manna in the wilderness which was bread from heaven.'"

"*They were looking for more signs?*" I asked incredulously.

"*Yes. Perhaps you have heard of the manna which appeared each day at dawn and lasted for only one day. This happened each day of the forty years that they spent wandering in the wilderness with Moses. When they entered the promised land, the manna no longer appeared.*"

"*No. I didn't know that,*" I said.

"*Then Yeshua said to them, 'it is my Father who gives you the true bread from heaven. For the bread of God is that which comes down from heaven and gives life to the world.' They said to him,*

Sir, give us this bread always.'

And then Yeshua said to them,

'I am the bread of life for I have come down from heaven. I am the bread of life. Whoever comes to me will never be hungry, and whoever believes in me will never be thirsty.'"

I was finding this difficult to understand. Why would Yeshua compare himself to bread? Isn't the bread we eat each day eaten to sustain life? Is God going to send us manna once again? Was Yeshua saying that he was the new manna? But he wasn't bread, he was a man. So, we couldn't eat him. And he didn't appear at dawn each day and then disappear like the manna. I was happy to believe that he was the Son of God and had come down from heaven. But he definitely was not bread of any kind.

Jonathan broke into my reverie. He suggested that I take a walk to reflect and I was happy to do this. He said that he would remain and prepare some lunch and that he would tell me more later.

"*Before you go, however, there are two matters I wish to relate and which you might mull on.*

Many centuries ago, Abram met with Melchizedek of Salem who brought out bread and wine to sacrifice; he was a priest of God Most High. Salem was probably Jerusalem.

At his last supper in Jerusalem Yeshua blessed bread and wine before going to sacrifice himself."

I smiled to myself, hmm, food for thought, indeed.

Lord, to whom can I go?

For some time, I sat by the spring which is the source of the river flowing down Terra Olivia. The gentle murmur of the water flowing over the rocks induced a state of reverie. And words swam aimlessly around in my head – bread, Yeshua, manna, lifeness, sacrifice, from heaven, true bread, Yeshua, eating bread, the bread of life, life…Sacrifice?

Jonathan arrived and sat beside me.

"*I don't know what all the fuss was about,*" I said. "*The mob was obviously impressed at the miraculous way in which he could feed so many with so little. Well, so am I. They probably wondered what else might he be able to do for them to make their lives easier. After all he said that he had come down from heaven. So, maybe they thought that he was the answer to their prayers in more ways than simply supplying bread.*"

Jonathan looked at me intently. '*I want you to stay with me while I tell you this. Will you?*"

What was he so apprehensive about, I wondered?

"*Yes, sure.*"

"*Yeshua then said to them,*

'I am the bread of life.

Your ancestors ate the manna in the wilderness, and they died.

This is the bread that comes down from heaven, so that one may eat of it and not die.

I am the living bread that came down from heaven.

Whoever eats of this bread will live forever,

Jonathan paused and whispered

and the bread that I will give for the life of the world

is my flesh'

I wasn't sure that I heard what he said correctly.

"*Pardon?*"

"*You heard me. He said that they were to eat his body. Don't be afraid. Stay with me, I will explain.*"

I wasn't afraid so much as shocked. He was talking about Yeshua, a kind and gentle man, a man who only did good things and who counselled his disciples to love one another. Did he mean to sacrifice himself by having us eat him. The thought was utterly repellent. What was this person, Jonathan, up to? But I knew that Yeshua died by crucifixion, he had not been eaten. Therefore, this was a tissue of lies by Jonathan. I was trembling from head to toe. I scrambled to my feet and furiously hurled my words at Jonathan,

"*Cannibalism! I don't believe you. Who are you? How can you utter such abominable and perfidious deceits? Get away from me. Get away."*

"*No Dónal. There is no cannibalism. Hear me out. Yeshua only ever did good. I will explain matters to you. I know that you are a fair man. Give me a few moments to explain matters to you. Please, Dónal."*

My shock was subsiding a little. My training as a news reporter kicked in and I decided that I would give him a hearing. Grudgingly, I confess.

"*Well?"*

"*Those listening to Yeshua had the same reaction as you and many of his disciples turned back and no longer went about with him. So, Yeshua asked the twelve,*

'*Do you also wish to go away?'*

Simon Peter answered him,

'*Lord, to whom can we go? You have the words of eternal life. We have come to believe and know that you are the Holy One of God.'*

Peter would have been as shocked as you are, Dónal but, like Abraham, he clung onto his faith and trust in God and gave us those immortal words that I cling to every time I am tempted to doubt,

Lord, to whom can I go?

Bear with me. I have mentioned to you Melchizedek who brought out bread and wine to sacrifice when he met Abram. Now I want to tell you of a particular command given by God to Moses when they reached the promised land."

I had calmed down somewhat by this time, but I felt that he was equivocating. Was he alleging that Yeshua asked his followers to eat him or not? I was not interested in what Moses did so many centuries ago.

"*You are stalling*" I said, "*are you alleging that Yeshua said to eat him or not?*"

"*I know you to be a fair man, Dónal. Just give me a hearing. There are some things you need to know in order to understand. For example, about the 'Bread of the Presence'''.*

More stalling, I thought. But I did like to be thought of as fair! "*Go on.*"

"*The Book of Leviticus tells us that God commanded Moses to*

'take choice flour and bake twelve loaves of it…place them in two rows, six in a row, on the table of pure gold before the Lord in the tabernacle…Every Sabbath day Aaron shall set them in order before the Lord regularly as a…covenant forever. They shall be for Aaron and his descendants, who shall eat them in a holy place, for they are most holy portions for him…to the Lord, a perpetual due.'

Since that time on every Sabbath the priests have placed bread on a golden altar at the door of the Tabernacle (the 'Holy of Holies') as a sacrifice to God. There were no blood sacrifices on the Sabbath. They then took the bread which had been sacrificed into the Tabernacle and ate it with wine. In fact, since before the time of Moses and before Abraham it was the custom to offer bread and wine to God."

Jonathan paused and looked at me. What did he expect? I mentally recapitulated:
- Melchizedek made a sacrifice of bread and wine eons ago;
- God sent bread in the form of manna for forty years;
- The Jewish priests sacrificed bread every week for hundreds of years.

- Yeshua said that he was the living bread who came down from heaven.
- Yeshua sacrificed himself.

But flesh is not bread. Flesh is flesh.

"All right, Jonathan. That is all very interesting. I have no problem with people offering bread to God or with people eating such bread. I do have a problem with people sacrificing a person to God. And I do have a problem with people then eating such a sacrifice. You have not said anything that would assuage my utter disgust at such a notion."

"Well, now I think I can help you to see how much more awesome Yeshua was than you think," said Jonathan.

"You have heard of the supper Yeshua shared with his disciples on the Thursday before he was crucified, haven't you?"

I had heard something in relation to this during my sessions with various groups of Christians when dining with them.

"Yes. His followers have a meal where they share bread and wine in memory of him."

"It is not simply a memorial", said Jonathan.

"What do you mean?"

"Just before his last supper with his disciples Yeshua said to them,

'I have eagerly desired to eat this Passover with you before I suffer'.

He knew that he was soon to endure scourging, crucifixion and death. Why should he be so eager about this particular meal?"

I didn't know why. Why would he eagerly desire to share a meal with others. Strong words, "eagerly" and "desire". Yeshua had been sharing meals with them for the past several years. What might be so special about this one I wondered? With no little journalistic conceit I answered,

"Something portentous was about to occur."

"Yes" said Jonathan beaming. *"Something portentous. Something amazing, life-changing, awe inspiring."*

I gaped at him, *"What?"*

"*You remember that Yeshua said,*
I am the Bread of Life
Come down from heaven".
"*Yes.*"
"And,
Whoever eats of this bread will live forever, and the bread that I will give for the life of the world is my flesh"
I just stared at him. I could feel a shiver run down my spine as a certain dread gripped me.
"*As soon as Yeshua said those words over the bread it was no longer bread.*"
"*I don't understand.*"
"*It was transformed into the living bread that had come down from heaven as Yeshua had said. It was transformed into Yeshua.*"[10]
"*Living bread?*" I squeaked.
"*You are thinking 'but Yeshua died', aren't you?*" asked Jonathan.
"*Yes.*"
"*Do you believe that he rose from the dead?*"
"*Yes.*"
"*And that he ascended into heaven?*"
"*Yes. He was with us for only a short time. And now we remember him when we share a meal and remember what he said on the night before he died.*"
And then I became aware that Nicodemus had arrived and was standing behind us.
We sat in silence for a while as I tried to absorb what he said.
"*Glory be*" said Nicodemus, "*the light is dawning for Dónal. Grace is flooding into you. You will now see that what still appeared to be bread was Yeshua. Body and soul and Divinity. Alive and with us. But, hidden. As Yeshua said to us, 'my flesh is true food, and my blood is true drink. Those who eat my flesh and drink my blood abide in me and I in them. Just as the living*

---

[10] See appendix on Thomas Aquinas' dissertation.

Father sent me and I live because of the Father so whoever eats me will live because of me'. As the angel Gabriel said to Mary:

'For nothing will be impossible with God".

I had to sit down again. I needed to think. But I couldn't. How could such a thing be possible? Then again, how could somebody who was dead rise to lifeness again? Did this concept throw doubt on everything else that Yeshua had said and done? How could what to all appearances of sight and taste was bread be a person, a person who had died, be God. Oops, here I was again, thinking like those Greek philosophers. My companions were waiting patiently and Nicodemus said,
"*Come let us go back to Kition and rest. Does not what you have now learned give meaning to the last words of Yeshua:*

'And remember, I am with you always, to the end of the age'".

The Alpha and the Omega.

"*Let us sit, Dónal, and I will try and set a context for you,*", said Nicodemus.

"*In the beginning, before the universe was created, was the Word. The Word was with God and the Word was God. All things came into being through him. What has come into being in him was life. Life. Lifeness. Life.*

Humans were created in the image of God and were created good. They were given the ability to think about their purpose in being brought into life and were given free will to choose how they would live.

But, from the beginning God, in his ineffable wisdom, permitted Satan, who is the father of lies, to test humans by trying to lure them away from their loving God. He was too strong for humans to oppose. He brought death into the world. For a long time, Satan was successful and humans offended their creator. Humankind failed - we needed help.

God intervened and chose one people, the Jews, to begin the exodus of all humans from the clutches of the evil one. He entered into covenants with this people, but despite these interventions the world lay under the power of the evil one. What could be done by mere humans to redress their offences against their creator? How could the finite make redress for offences against the Infinite? It was not possible.

But, as the angel Gabriel said to Mary, 'for nothing will be impossible with God'.

And so, the Word became flesh and lived among us bringing God's kingdom near to our world. And his name is Yeshua. Now what to us seemed impossible happened. One man living on Earth was God. And all changed, changed utterly."

Jonathan continued. "*Yeshua manifested his infinite love for us by suffering the most awful death imaginable. He rose from the death state and showed us that, notwithstanding our deaths in this life, we also are immortal. He ascended, body,* soul and Divinity into heaven to be our advocate with the Father until the end of time. But, also he comes to us daily in the forms of bread and wine and cohabits with us to nourish and develop our spiritual life and will do so until the end of time."

Nicodemus handed me a scroll. "*This is a draft of writings by John the apostle. Retire to your room and read it. It contains much of what Jonathan has told you. Meditate and pray. We will meet again in a day or two.*"

I enjoyed two days of peace mesmerized by the spiritual treasures unveiled for us by John and reflected on my journey to Truth. I had approached the followers of Yeshua with deep suspicion looking for an ulterior motive behind their existence in numerous small groups throughout the empire. Not to put too fine a point on it, with tunnel vision. It was quite mortifying and humbling to identify this biased attitude on my part – I who supposedly was "*the intrepid reporter fearlessly seeking the truth*"!

But now I could see that had I not fallen victim to misfortunes I might never have come to the truth. Oh, the paradox of how apparent misfortunes steered me to the good fortune of the Truth. And, I may say, steered me in spite of myself - how mysterious are your ways, Lord. To think that I had met with Peter, the Lord's appointed representative on Earth, and Paul who was visited by Yeshua and became the apostle to the gentiles. How fortunate to meet with Clement and Nicodemus. How could I ever thank God for such wondrous blessings, I wondered. I was soon to find out!

Reflection – Life and Eternal Life.

Alone in my room I, the fearless reporter, wrote down:

Yeshua's actions:

Multiplying five loaves to feed more than five thousand people
A Theophany of walking on water and quelling a storm.

Yeshua's reminder:

God provided manna from heaven to sustain human life for forty years until the promised land was reached.

Yeshua's plea:

Do not work for the food that perishes but for the food that endures for eternal life, which the Son of Man will give you.

Yeshua's validation:

I have come from the Father and
Very truly, I tell you, whoever believes has eternal life.

What Yeshua wants us to believe:

I am the bread of **life**
I have come down from heaven
I am the **living bread** that came down from heaven.
The bread that I will give for the **life** of the world is my flesh.
Unless you eat the flesh of the Son of Man and drink his blood, you have no **life** in you.
Those who eat my flesh and drink my blood abide in me and I in them.
Those who eat my flesh and drink my blood have **eternal life.**

Later at the last supper:

Then Yeshua took a loaf of bread, and when he had given thanks, he broke it and gave it to them, saying, "This is my body, which is given for you. Do this in remembrance of me"
And he did the same with the cup after supper.

At Emmaus:

When he was at the table with them, he took bread, blessed and broke it, and gave it to them. Then their eyes were opened, and they recognized him.

To Thomas:
"Blessed are those who have not seen and yet have come to believe."

Feeding more than five thousand people by multiplying five loaves was a mind-boggling miraculous deed – a visible one. Yeshua showed visibly what he could do with bread. This was a portent of what he would do invisibly with bread – with the *"staff of life"*. So that the staff of earthly life would become the staff of eternal life? Yeshua says that the bread is his body and that we are to eat it in order to have eternal life. My bodily senses will not let me apprehend his presence. I need the gift of Faith to believe it. And God will give me that grace if I ask for it.

I knelt and prayed. Yeshua had died. But, the hour of his death was, as he had said during his last supper with his disciples, the hour of his glorification. His body in the Eucharist is different from the way his body was when he walked about Judea. It is his glorified body as it became after his resurrection and ascension. It is a glorified body no longer limited by matter, time or space. It is this glorified body, soul and divinity that we receive in the Eucharist. His glorified body, that at the same as I receive it, is in the immediate presence of God for *"we have an advocate with the Father, Jesus Christ the righteous."*

Nicodemus said that while it still appears to be bread – it looks and tastes like bread – the substance of bread has been replaced by the presence of Yeshua so that it is no longer bread. I wonder about that. Some people had said something similar about Yeshua. They suggested that he only appeared to be a human but was in fact the Son of God – one couldn't be a human and God at the same time. Such a view was held by the elders to be in error – Yeshua was both a human and God. So, couldn't the Host be both bread and Yeshua? It doesn't really matter to me since either way Yeshua is really and actually present. But Nicodemus disabused me of this notion – there was only Jesus, body, soul and Divinity. As the angel Gabriel said:

"For nothing will be impossible with God."

I humbly thank God for *"shining His light on what we need to know"*. My life has taken on a new meaning.

Life
One God,
My father,
Cares for me.
I will live for Him
I will live for Him for eternity.

Publisher's note:
What kind of presence is there in the Eucharist?
Christians have four differing views:
1. A **symbolic** commemoration of the Last Supper. This is true, but only part of the whole truth.
2. A **spiritual** presence indwelling the bread and wine.
3. What occurs is what is termed "***consubstantiation***". This originated with Martin Luther who believed that the body and blood of Jesus were present along **with** the bread and wine.
4. Catholics believe in the "*Real Presence*" of Jesus, body and soul and Divinity under the appearances of bread and wine. There is no longer bread or wine – there is only glorified Jesus. Theologians call this "*transubstantiation*", a doctrine enunciated at the Council of Trent (1543 -1563).

Foundation stones.

In late afternoon on the third day Clement along with the other residents of our compound took me to the river Maroni. And there he baptized me. I, Dónal Clement Quaestor, became a Christian. That evening at the communal meal I received Yeshua into my body. I will not attempt to describe my enraptured state of mind at that time. Afterwards a tincture of what might have been pride made its way into my consciousness.

I, Dónal, was the first Hibernian to become a Christian.

But, was it pride or an inkling of what was to unfold?
There was in our compound at that time a man named Timon. He had come from Jerusalem. He was a man of good standing, full of the Spirit and of wisdom. With six others he had been appointed by the apostles to look after day to day matters for the community while the apostles devoted themselves to prayer and to serving the Word. He had set up a similar housekeeping group in Kition. I was appointed to join this group and I stood before Clement and Nicodemus who prayed and laid their hands on me.

It was very beneficial for me, the erstwhile centre of the universe, to be the servant of all. Also, Nicodemus became my mentor instructing me in the Tanak so that I might better understand how the coming of our Messiah had been foreshadowed for centuries in the Law and the Prophets which he had come, not to abolish, but to fulfil.

I wasn't sure that I wanted to spend my time learning the history of the Jews – I wanted to know more about Yeshua.

"*You need to walk before you can run*", he said. "*On the day of his resurrection Yeshua appeared to two despondent disciples as they trudged home following the death of Yeshua. And he said to them,*

'Oh, how foolish you are and how slow of heart to believe all that the prophets have declared! Was it not necessary that the Messiah should suffer these things and then enter into his glory?'

Then beginning with Moses and all the prophets, he interpreted to them the things about himself in all the scriptures. It was following this that their eyes were opened and they recognized him. And that is what we must do, Dónal."

So, that was what we did. As he said, my eyes were opened. Nicodemus continued.

"*We, Christians of the Jewish and gentile races, are of the Jewish religion as fulfilled by Yeshua. Like Paul we are New Covenant Jews. Most of what were temporary laws in Deuteronomy and Ecclesiastes are no longer relevant. But some are, for example the ten commandments. And the long-awaited Messiah has arrived as an infinitely greater gift from God than the one foreseen by Daniel and the prophets. He remains with us as the Bread of Life come down from the Father, and, with the Advocate guiding us through Peter and his successors so that we will remain in the Truth.*"

What a consolation this is I thought as I recalled how, several years ago, Peter and the elders were guided to see that Yeshua came, not just for the chosen people, but for all peoples of the world.

As I sat musing Clement came to me.

"*I have an assignment for you, Dónal. You are to go to John the apostle who will give you a mission. You will leave tomorrow.*"

"*Yes, Clement. I will gladly go. Where is John and what is the mission?*"

"*John is on the island of Patmós, a long journey from here. He will instruct you on your mission. Take this letter with you and deliver it to John.*"

This would indeed be a long journey. But it would afford me time to further meditate on the Tanakh and some writings concerning Yeshua. And time to update my journal.

Patmós.

Patmós is a small island situated in the Aegean Sea a short distance off the west coast of the Asia Minor. It took me nearly three months to journey to Patmós.

John was living in one of the caves half way up the island's mountain. His disciples also lived in the caves and I was allotted one of the caves. One of his followers, Ignatius, told me that the risen, glorified Son of God appeared to John and commanded him to write "*the things that you have seen, those that are and those that are to take place after this.*" He had retired to Patmós to complete this apocalyptic work before he went to his heavenly reward.

It was with no little trepidation that I met with John the following day. This was the man who as a naïve youth wanted "*to sit on the right hand of Yeshua*", who witnessed the raising to life of Jairus' daughter, witnessed the Transfiguration, witnessed the agony of Yeshua in the garden, witnessed the crucifixion, and became a son to Mary. I was standing in the presence of greatness. I wasn't terrified – but I was close to being so. Bowing my head I gave him the letter from Clement. He smiled and, laying the letter aside, took my hand in both of his.

"*Welcome, brother Dónal*" he said. I realised that I had all of his attention. I felt that he looked into my soul and saw everything. I trusted him unreservedly. Although he was now old, he had the same vitality as I imagined he had had when he outran Peter in a race to the empty tomb. I was captivated and could say nothing so I merely nodded my head.

Eventually, "*sit, Dónal,*" he said. And we sat.

"*Let us pray to the Holy Ghost for guidance in our endeavours.*

Oh, Holy God give us wisdom to discern the path of life you wish Dónal to follow. Help us to see clearly the things that matter and the things that don't. Help him to use every gift he has, remembering that it is from you.

He opened the letter from Clement and read it. He smiled. "*Clement is of the same mind as me. I cannot say it better than:*

'*Go therefore and make disciples of the Gaels of Hibernia, baptizing them in the name of the Father and of the Son and of the Holy Ghost, and teaching them to obey everything that Yeshua has commanded us. And remember, Yeshua is with you always, to the end of the age.*'

As you will understand I was bewildered. Immediately I recalled that tiny barb of pride when I extolled myself as the first Hibernian to have been baptized. Was this the reason for thinking of my homeland at that moment, I asked myself? Surely, they would kill me as soon as I set foot on Hibernian soil.

My face must have given away my negative thoughts.

"*I understand, Dónal. You are right to feel much trepidation. You are not the first person to say, 'my Father, if it is possible, let this cup pass from me'. It is indeed possible for you to eschew the cup, Dónal. But if you do not go we shall lose many as we wait for another messenger. I hope that you say, 'yet, not as I will, but as you will'.*"

I can tell you that there were a lot of negative thoughts swirling in my head. We sat in silence for some time. John is as patient as Clement, I thought. I couldn't think coherently. Most of the thoughts I came up with started "*but*" *and there were several that started* "*I want,*" *and* "*I wish*". *And a probing one I couldn't banish no matter how hard I tried:*

"*I am not the centre of the universe*".

"*Dónal*". *I was plucked back into reality by John.* "*Just pray, Dónal. You have been presented with a difficult calling. I foresee that you will not have great success in terms of the number who will become Christians during your lifetime.*

You will be one calling in the wilderness and making the path straight for the ones who will come after you.
Did not John do great work for God even if nobody became a Christian before he died? Did not Yeshua say of him, 'Truly I tell you, among those who are born of women no one has arisen greater than John the Baptist?"

Perspective, I thought. I need time to get everything in perspective.

John obviously agreed for he said to me,

"*You should go now to your cave and pray. Meditate on what we have discussed. I have adapted Psalm 67 slightly in the hope that it may be of assistance."*

He handed me a small scroll. When I got back to my dwelling I unfurled it and read:

May God be gracious to the Gaels and bless them
And make his face shine on them
So that your ways may be known among all.
May they praise you, God;
may all the Hibernians praise you.
May they be glad and sing for joy,
For you rule all peoples with equity
and guide the nations of the earth.
May the peoples praise you, God;
may all the peoples praise you.
The land yields its harvest;
God, our God, blesses us.

Vacillation and Resolve.

What was my first thought when I got back to my lodging?
"*Yes. I will go fearlessly forth and bring the Good News to my Hibernian brothers and sisters*"?
No!
Satan was at work with suggestions:
I am definitely not like John the Baptist;
I'm sure that Yeshua never heard of Hibernia;
Hadn't I had to flee from there when the Druids issued a warrant for my death?;
Waste of a resource (me) going to Hibernia since I would probably be killed before I could achieve anything;
I have a good knowledge of Rome and know many influential Romans and so I could be more fruitful there;
The Druids are too strong a dominating influence.
The Druids have divinised nature.
Nature.
Then it hit me.
What do Hibernians love?
They love Nature and stories.
And how did Yeshua convey his message to us?
Stories:

A sower went out to sow…
The seed would sprout and grow, he does not know how…
When sown upon the ground the mustard seed is the smallest of all, but…
Look at the birds of the air…
Consider the lilies of the field…
While everybody was asleep an enemy came and sowed weeds among the wheat…
The shepherd and the sheep…
The unforgiving servant…
The labourers in the vineyard…
The prodigal son…
The two sons and their promises…

The talents...
The good Samaritan...
The dishonest steward...
The judge and the persistent widow...
The Pharisee and the tax collector...
The shamrock...!

Confounding the arrogant intelligentsia.
Render unto Caesar....
Showing the Sadducees how little they knew of the scriptures or God...
How could royal King David say that his descendant, Yeshua was his Lord?
Why do you see the speck in your neighbour's eye...
Know that a tree is good by its fruit...
And stories from the Tanakh.
Adam and Eve and the serpent...
Moses and exodus...
David and Goliath...
Job...
Oh, how delighted my kinsfolk would be to have all this made known to them. And so much more. And I remembered some things that Clement had said to me:
 "Fear not, Dónal. You have won favour with our Lord. He will hold you in his hand and you shall not perish."
And:
"I shall call you in time to come.
I have a task for you."
Was he prescient. Was my initially sceptical focus on Christians, my enslavement along with Clement, my shipwreck- again along with Clement and my meetings with Nicodemus accidents or parts of God's plan?
Oops! There's that question again:
"*Is it possible?*"
Then in my mind's eye I saw...

I would love to see again the land of my birth and early life. I have a spiritual and a human reason to go home.

> *I will arise and go now, for always night and day*
> *I hear its waters lapping with low sounds by the shore;*
> *While I stand on Patmós, or anywhere in Rome,*
> *I hear it in my deep heart's core.*

I had started my life's work with the aim of "*Shining a spotlight on what citizens need to know*". Until now everything has been as dust is to diamonds. Now I could bring Truth and God to my kinsfolk. There was nothing greater that I could do.

Slán agus Beannacht libh go léir.

I met with John and told him of my decision. When we gathered for supper that night, he asked me to give his followers an account of my life. I did this very briefly and told them that they could learn more in the journal that I would leave with them. John then informed all of my mission. He then ordered me to lie prostrate before all and he consecrated me bishop and priest. It was all too much for me emotionally and, I shamedly confess, that I broke down and cried. That was all right because I was among loving friends and brothers in Christ. John then asked for volunteers who would accompany me on and share in my mission.

Over the next several days we made preparations for our long voyage and gathered together various tools and items that would be helpful in our dialogues with the Hibernians.

Today, along with five other missionaries, I am to set sail for home and, in closing my journal, ask you to pray for us.

Pax vobiscum sit,
Dónal Clement Quaestor.
May 69 C.E.

THE END.

Publishers' note.

St. Brendan was born in Tralee, county Kerry in 484 C.E. From notes in his journal, we have been able to gather the following information.

Dónal and his fellow pilgrims landed at the Ciarraighe peninsula which is situated at the south-west of Hibernia. The land was owned and populated by tribes called O'Sullivan, O'Connor, Shea, Murphy, McCarthy. Dónal and his fellow missionaries were allowed to occupy a small portion of bogland and built a monastery there which is named *"An Riasc"*.

Progress in *"spreading the Word"* was very slow due to the constant interference of the Druids and their minions. Several other centres were built along the western and southern coasts but they were in constant peril.

What was significant, however, was the way in which the parables were spread by the *seanchaithe*, albeit often with variations, among families around the *tinteáin* at night.

Although, after some twenty years, Dónal was betrayed and assassinated by Frídín O'Fealltóir it was Dónal who *"made straight the way of the Lord"* for future missionaries. It was he who, as the Lord God ordered from the beginning, tilled the ground for Patrick and the rest of us.

Appendix 1

Forgiveness.
Gospels

	Mark
1:4	John the baptizer appeared in the wilderness, proclaiming a baptism of repentance **for the forgiveness of sins**.
2:5	When Jesus saw their faith, he said to the paralytic, "**Child, your sins are forgiven**."
3:28	Truly I tell you, people will **be forgiven for their sins**
11:25	"Whenever you stand praying, **forgive**, if you have anything against anyone, so that your Father in heaven may also **forgive** you your trespasses."
	Matthew
4:17	At the beginning of his ministry: From that time Jesus began to proclaim, "*Repent, for the kingdom of heaven has come near.*"
5:7	"*Blessed are the merciful, for they will receive mercy*"
5:25	"*So when you are offering your gift at the altar, if you remember that your brother or sister has something against you, leave your gift there before the altar and go;* **first be reconciled** *to your brother or sister, and then come and offer your gift.*"
5:43	"*You have heard that it was said, 'You shall love your neighbour and hate your enemy.' But I say to you: Love your enemies and pray for those who persecute you, so that you may be children of your Father in heaven..."*
6:9	"And **forgive us**

	our debts, as we also have forgiven our debtors."
6:14	"*For if you **forgive** others their trespasses, your heavenly Father will also **forgive** you, but if you do not **forgive** others, neither will your Father **forgive** your trespasses.*"
7:1	"Do not judge, so that you may not be judged. For the judgment you give will be the judgment you get, and **the measure you give will be the measure you get.**"
9:2	When Jesus saw their faith, he said to the paralytic, "*Take heart, child;* **your sins are forgiven.**"
9:13	"*Go and learn what this means,* '**I desire mercy**, *not sacrifice*"
10:8	"You received without payment; give without payment."
11:20	Then he began to reproach the cities in which most of his deeds of power had been done **because they did not repent**… "*I tell you, on the day of judgment it will be more tolerable for Tyre and Sidon than for you.*"
18:21	Then Peter came and said to him, "*Lord, if my brother or sister sins against me,* **how often should I forgive?** *As many as seven times?*" Jesus said to him, "*Not seven times, but, I tell you, **seventy-seven times**.*"
18:32	'*You wicked slave!* **I forgave you** *all that debt because you pleaded with me. Should you not have had mercy on your fellow slave, as I had mercy on you?*' *So my heavenly Father will also do to every one of*

	you, *if you do not* *forgive your brother or sister from your heart."* See also prayer given by Yeshua: "*forgive us* *our trespasses* **as we forgive those** *who trespass against us".*
26:26	*"Take, eat; this is my body."* Then he took a cup, and after giving thanks he gave it to them, saying, *"Drink from it, all of you, for this is my blood of the covenant, which is poured out for many* **for the forgiveness of sins."**

Luke

1:76	*"for you will go before the Lord to prepare his ways, to give his people knowledge of salvation by the* **forgiveness of their sins."**
3:3	He went into all the region around the Jordan, proclaiming a **baptism of repentance for the forgiveness of sins**
5:20	When he saw their faith, he said, "Friend, **your sins are forgiven you.**"
5:32	*"I have not come to call the righteous but* **sinners to repentance."**
6:27	"If anyone strikes you on the cheek, offer the other also... Give to everyone who asks of you, and if anyone takes away what is yours, do not ask for it back again. Do to others as you would have them do to you."
6:36	*"Be merciful, just as your Father is merciful."*
6:37	"***Forgive,*** *and you will be forgiven*"
Lk 7:47	"...I tell you, her many sins have been forgiven; hence she has shown great love. But the one to whom little

	is forgiven loves little."
7:48	Then he said to her, "*Your sins are **forgiven**.*"
11:4	*"And **forgive** us our sins, for we ourselves **forgive** everyone indebted to us."*
23:34	Then Jesus said, *"Father **forgive them**, for they do not know what they are doing."*
24:44	*"Thus it is written, that the Messiah is to suffer and to rise from the dead on the third day and that repentance and **forgiveness of sins** is to be proclaimed in his name to all nations…"*
John	
20:22	*'Peace be with you. As the Father has sent me, so I send you.' When he had said this, he breathed on them and said to them, 'Receive the Holy Spirit. If you **forgive** the sins of any, they are forgiven them; if you retain the sins of any, they are retained.'*

Appendix 2.

Excerpt from Summa Theologica of St. Thomas Aquinas.
[*Emphasises mine!*]

76. The Real Presence

1. In the Holy Eucharist, Christ is present whole and entire (**body, blood, soul, and Godhead or divinity**) under the appearances or accidentals of bread and wine.
The words of consecration (which constitute the *form* of the sacrament of Holy Eucharist) bring the **living** Christ, God and man, truly present. The words, "This is my body," bring Christ's body truly present. This is Christ's *living* body; therefore, it has its blood, its soul, and the Godhead which assumed this body. The words, "This is my blood," bring Christ's blood truly present. This is Christ's *living* blood; therefore it is in its body, with the soul, and the divinity or Godhead which has assumed this blood. Thus, the whole Christ is present under the appearances of bread, and the whole Christ is present under the appearances of wine, and the whole Christ is present under both appearances together. For, if two things are really united, wherever one is the other must be. And Christ's complete humanity (in its elements of body, blood, and soul) is really united with his divinity.
Thus, by the power of this sacrament, the body of Christ is present at the words, "This is my body," and, by the *necessity of concomitance,* the blood of Christ is present also, as is the soul, and the divinity. And the blood of Christ is present at the words, "This is my blood," and, by the necessity of concomitance, the body of Christ is present also, as is the soul, and the divinity.
2. Therefore, the whole Christ, God and man, is contained under each *species*-that is, each set of appearances, namely, the appearances of bread, and the appearances of wine.

3. And the whole Christ is present under every part or quantity of each species. As a loaf of bread is *bread,* and a slice of bread is *bread,* and a crumb of bread is *bread,* so, the Eucharistic species, in whatever quantity, is Christ.

There is a difference, however, in the fact that Christ is not diminished as the bread is diminished when the loaf is taken and a slice is left, or when a slice is taken away and only a crumb is left. Christ is not made smaller as the species becomes smaller, but is whole and entire (entirely unaffected by any external dimensions) in any tangible quantity of the consecrated *matter* (that is, bread and wine).

4. The whole dimensive quantity of Christ's body is present in every particle of the Eucharistic species (every crumb, every drop), but Christ's body has not its external extension or dimensions. Nor is Christ's body measured, and "sized," according to the amounts and measurements of the species of bread and wine. The dimensions of the species are accidentals of the species; they do not become the dimensions of Christ. But **the dimensions of Christ are present** after the manner in which the substance of Christ is present, that is, complete in each particle, as bread is complete bread in each loaf, and slice, and crumb. The size of the sacred host is not the size of Christ; nor is Christ present in miniature, or as cramped under a quantity of the species; **he is present whole and entire, and in full stature**, but that stature is not *externally* measured or dimensioned.

5. Christ's body is not in this sacrament as a body is in *a place.* For a body in a place is there according to its external dimensions, and these make the body commensurate with the dimensions of the place it occupies. But Christ's body is not present in the Eucharist according to external dimensions. His body is present *quantitatively,* not in the manner of the external accidentals of measurement and dimension, but according to the manner of substance, which is complete in any quantity, large or small, that exists.

6. Our Lord is not present in a *movable* way in the Holy Eucharist.

Only a body that is *located* (that is, is in a place according to external dimensions), can be moved from place to place. Hence, when the Eucharistic species is moved, Christ is not moved. If the sacred host be dropped, Christ does not fall down. If the sacred host be moved from right to left, from left to right, or raised or lowered, Christ himself is not thus moved about. Christ is not subject to local movement, even though the sacramental species are so subject.

7. The body of Christ in the Blessed Sacrament, as the Holy Eucharist is lovingly called, cannot be seen by any eye, even the eye of a glorified body. The glorified eye sees Christ in his own proper species, as he is in heaven since the day of Ascension. No eye can see Christ as he is present in the Holy Eucharist. **Christ is seen there by the mind, the intellect, illumined by faith.** The *glorified* intellect (in heaven) sees all supernatural things in its view of the beatific vision of God.

8. When, by an apparition, flesh or blood is seen in the sacred host, this is not the actual flesh and blood of Christ. The actual flesh and blood of Christ is present, but invisible. The apparition is an apparition, not a reality. The blood that is seen to flow from a consecrated host (as a miraculous manifestation) is not Christ's own blood, which is never shed again after the Passion. Such a manifestation is a fearsome reminder to the observers to be aware of the *real* blood of Christ present in the host *invisibly*.

See also:
Catechism of the Catholic Church
sections 1373 to 1378.

1273 C.E.

Thomas Aquinas] was celebrating Mass when he received a revelation that so affected him that he wrote and dictated no more, leaving his great work the *Summa Theologiae* unfinished. To Brother Reginald's (his secretary and friend) expostulations he replied,

"The end of my labours has come.

All that I have written appears to be as so much straw after the things that have been revealed to me."

Appendix 3.
Nicene Creed as amended by Council of Constantinople.

I believe in one God, the Father almighty,
maker of heaven and earth,
of all things visible and invisible.
I believe in one Lord Jesus Christ,
the Only Begotten Son of God,
born of the Father before all ages.
God from God, Light from Light,
true God from true God,
begotten, not made, consubstantial
with the Father;
Through him all things were made.
For us men and for our salvation
he came down from heaven,
and by the Holy Spirit was incarnate
of the Virgin Mary,
and became man.
For our sake he was crucified
under Pontius Pilate,
he suffered death and was buried,
and rose again on the third day
in accordance with the Scriptures.
He ascended into heaven
and is seated at the right hand of the Father.
He will come again in glory
to judge the living and the dead
and his kingdom will have no end.
I believe in the Holy Spirit,
the Lord, the giver of life,
who proceeds from the Father and the Son,
who with the Father and the Son
is adored and glorified,

who has spoken through the prophets.
I believe in one, holy, catholic,
and apostolic Church.
I confess one baptism for the forgiveness of sins
and I look forward to the resurrection
of the dead and the life of the world to come.
Amen.

Apostles' Creed.

I believe in God,
the Father almighty,
Creator of heaven and earth,
and in Jesus Christ, his only Son, our Lord,
who was conceived by the Holy Spirit,
born of the Virgin Mary,
suffered under Pontius Pilate,
was crucified, died and was buried;
he descended into hell;
on the third day he rose again from the dead;
he ascended into heaven,
and is seated at the right hand of God the Father almighty;
from there he will come to judge the living and the dead.

I believe in the Holy Spirit,
the holy catholic Church,
the communion of saints,
the forgiveness of sins,
the resurrection of the body,
and life everlasting.

Amen.

> This creed is thought to have been developed from initial interrogations of catechumens, people receiving instructions to be baptized.

Printed in Great Britain
by Amazon